PRAISE FOR J.

"James Sale is the grandmaster of high epic in our times."

— ANDREW BENSON BROWN, AUTHOR OF
LEGENDS OF LIBERTY

"Bravo... an achievement that will last for centuries, just as Dante's has."

— PROFESSOR JOSEPH SALEMI

"What this poem achieves is astonishing. [James Sale has] taken a personal tragedy and magnified it into an issue of cosmic proportion and done so organically and with superb taste."

— BRIAN YAPKO, AUTHOR OF *EL NUEVO MUNDO*

"A rollercoaster of a breathtaking ride through the dark realms of despair and loathing to the beauty and release of forgiveness and love. ... I know I've read a masterpiece."

— SUSAN JARVIS BRYANT, WINNER OF THE 2020 INTERNATIONAL SCP POETRY COMPETITION AND PUSHCART PRIZE NOMINEE

"A narrative of deepest feeling and boldest imagination ... Such memorable images!"

— JULIAN D WOODRUFF

"As with Dante, most remarkably of all ... has a representative quality in enacting the evil of what has occurred but not without compassion for the perpetrators, who (as usual but not always) did not understand the meaning of what they did at the time they did it ."

— DR. TOM WOODMAN

"Thank you for your wonderful poem. It made me think of our world today and the mercy and hope at the end was good for my soul."

— ALLEGRA SILBERSTEIN

"I was entranced by your allegory that must rank with the all-time great classical poet masters, but even more than that an epic of immense proportions ... should be read in Parliament and Congress in addition to the highest elected leaders and officials."

— ROY EUGENE PETERSON, AUTHOR OF
THE VELVETHAMMER

STAIRWELL

THE ENGLISH CANTOS VOL. II

JAMES SALE

Thank you for your stedfast
support Francis —
God bless you on your
journey to Paradiso !

Sale
23/4/23

First published 2023 © 2023 James Sale

The right of James Sale to be identified as authors of this work has been asserted by them in accordance with sections 77 and 78 of the Copyright, Designs and Patents Act 1988.

ISBN: 9798377514015

Printed and bound by Amazon KDP

Cover artwork "From The Well" by Linda E. Sale. Cover designed by Joseph Sale.

❀ Created with Vellum

To Professor Antonino Chiaramonte, musician, tutor and friend

"Non v'accorgete voi che noi siam vermi
nati a formar l'angelica farfalla,
che vola a la giustizia sanza schermi?

Di che l'animo vostro in alto galla,
poi siete quasi antomata in difetto,
sì come vermo in cui formazion falla?"

— *PURGATORY*, CANTO X, DANTE
ALIGHIERI

"Call upon Me on the day of trouble; I will rescue you,
and you will honour Me."

— PSALM 50 V15

"It is precisely this hyperreal meta-world that consists of
the continual interactions between chaos and order, which
eternally serve as the battleground between good and evil
characterising the hero."

— JORDAN B PETERSON, *BEYOND ORDER*

CONTENTS

FOREWORD

After first reading excerpts of *StairWell*, which were to be published by the Society of Classical Poets, I commented to the author James Sale, "Dante has gone down in history for his representation of hell in his Inferno. I think you will go down in history for your purgatory."

Let me backtrack a bit. The book you are now reading picks up as the second installment of James Sale's English Cantos trilogy, mirroring in many ways the epic trilogy of Dante Alighieri (1265-1351) within his *Divine Comedy*. Dante took us from hell to purgatory to heaven with his Inferno, Purgatorio, and Paradiso. Dante's real life experience of being exiled from his native Florence by Pope Boniface VIII in the 14th century was the backdrop for the intellectual fantasy adventure that ensued.

In James Sale's epic trilogy he has already taken us down to hell in his *HellWard* and we now journey upward through the 10 giant steps of *StairWell*, corresponding to the realm of purgatory. Instead of Dante's political exile, the critical real life experience is

James Sale's real battle with cancer—a battle which he has won and lived to tell about.

The intellectual fantasy adventure we get thanks to James Sale is certainly standing on the shoulders of giants; that is, building on the creative genius of Dante Alighieri (indeed, Dante plays a key role in the English Cantos as the guide). More importantly however, James Sale is bringing giants to your doorstep. He has written a story that is far more relatable to us here in the early 21st century than what Dante wrote 700 years ago. In Canto 4 of *Stair-Well* for instance, we encounter a high-tech society described in glittering language:

> The architecture, flash metals and cords
> Of twisted wire suspend—like massive limbs
> Heaving their own trunk upwards—a huge high road
> That purposes drive-throughs to paradise

This offers an immediately engaging setting. It is one that our hero encounters and it is also one that we encounter on a daily basis— you may very well be reading these words on a screen right now. Is it good? Is it bad? What do we make of it? James Sale's epic becomes our own life story as well, leaving room for stirring contemplations such these:

> How bright the future seems from where one stands
> Stuck in a present where light most seems dim;
> How little faith we have in now—beyond
> Is better, always there where we must climb

Another uniquely modern experience to connect with in *Stair-Well* is James Sale's encounter with his ex-wife in Canto 3. The awkwardness and painfulness of divorces and modern family relations is brought to life in a way more real than merely a straight memoir. After his ex-wife berates him, he writes:

> With that—her ominous first step towards me—
> I tensed, treading backwards, in total fear,
> My wretched mind revolving desperately
>
> Like some wasp buzzing in a locked jam jar,
> Below it, perilous waters waiting patient—
> And all I did not want looming so near

Notice how his rhymes act like feet also "treading backwards" with space between.

In another scene that strikes so near to home as to enter immediately into modern legend, James Sale and his guides are accosted by, of all people, a priest harping on about social distancing rules during the unforgettable pandemic years:

> Whose voice was this with its imperious lilt
> And caustic accusation? And there she was,
> As if up from an altar where she dwelt—
>
> Then magicked into our presence, alas!
> 'I am the priest in charge—Penny Crow—
> Where have you been, and have you had the vax?'

With this blisteringly honest storytelling, James Sale takes head on a theme that has risen to forefront of our world today. Namely, where has the faith and true spirituality gone in our modern life? It has gradually vanished while the world's ills—whether psychological, social, economic, or globally catastrophic—have seemed to gradually increase. Faith in a great and good Creator, in a higher power in the traditional sense of good over evil, is a distant second (or nothing at all) for many people in comparison to the almighty idol known as *The* Science (*The* Science, by the way, being a bastardization of a rational scientific search for Truth). To explain this fully becomes highly theoretical and deserves a book on its own as the issue is so complex. Instead, James Sale has captured the zeitgeist of what societies around the world have experienced, and he does it so succinctly and entertainingly with the "Covid-Priest" as he calls her. This is one of the great powers of poetry that James Sale has put to perfect use.

This brings me to another of the great powers of poetry, which is to create a sort of super-reality, or "licensed zone of hyper-reality" as I have heard the poet Joseph S. Salemi call it. For convenience and understandability, in the above, I have referred to a distinction between the real life event in James Sale's life, his battle with cancer, and used it in contrast to the intellectual fantasy adventure that constitutes most of his epic poem. However, psychological and spiritual adventures are no less real life events. Further, the term "fantasy" implies fiction, which is not accurate. When William Shakespeare wrote "Shall I compare thee to a summer's day?" he was engaging in a real mental process involving, presumably, a real person and all of the associated psychological impressions and feelings he had of this person as compared to those he had of a summer's day. The comparison was real and not a fantasy. We may even call it super real because it is dealing directly with first-hand mental experiences rather than any suppositions about the objective world. Therefore, we can call the epic poetry of James Sale and other epic writers super reality.

This is significant because so much of what is popular today in storytelling, movies, TV series, and novels, is complete fiction and as a result is not taken as intellectually serious. You have academic journals on one end of the spectrum and science fiction and fantasy movies on the other. When done well, an epic poem like *StairWell* has the gravitas and realness of an academic journal but, as you will find, a page-turning action-packed sense of adventure. To put it another way, you can have your cake and eat it too as long as the cake is a multi-dimensional epic poem.

> Just read these words from the first page of *StairWell*.
> Where was I, and where had I been before?
> Perched on a ledge now and somewhere between
> The hopeless dead with nothing to live for—
>
> For their own actions hold them self-condemned—
> And this place where my soles felt scorching heat
> Whilst in my face a cold blast cruelly thrummed.

Are these words describing a state of mind or an actual physical scene? Why not both? Just as Shakespeare can compare a person to a summer's day, James Sale takes us on a real 21st century adventure of the mind like nothing you've ever read before.

—Evan Mantyk,
President and Founder of The Society of Classical Poets

CANTO 1: ASCENT

The Argument

The poet has now escaped Hell, and has arrived in Purgatory or what he calls the StairWell. But he seems to have been abandoned by Dante, and has a fresh set of problems to confront. In this first section of the canto, he encounters an unexpected visitor from antiquity to help him on his way. One of the great gods who is really a Cherubim arrives to help them break through, facilitating a remarkable healing transformation. At last, a familiar friend re-joins their party to ascend the ten stairs of StairWell.

Some force, unknown before, but light as words
Are light, when sung beside alpine moraines
One sunny morning, clear, as those small birds

Their tweets ring for miles, echoing again
Eternal joy in that sheer riff of life

Which advertises nothing's been in vain.

So, then, I felt; or as the day my wife
Said yes and loneliness was all foregone
And so in joining her no more the strife

That's being two: forever we are one; $_{10}$
And thinking that one word, One, caused me then
To tremble: sure, another urged me on,

Awaiting with patience knowing no end
At last the demon in me would be cast
Out—to be finally home with all true men.

Yet, how could that be, for I was lost?
Within, too, cancer nipped, as crabs might do,
Their pincers picking, probing to digest

What flesh is, leaving only residue
Like litter laid on ocean's sweeping floor $_{20}$
And I, in all that swell, at last mere spew.

Where was I, and where had I been before?
Perched on a ledge now and somewhere between
The hopeless dead with nothing to live for—

For their own actions hold them self-condemned—
And this place where my soles felt scorching heat
Whilst in my face a cold blast cruelly thrummed.

I barely could see, no more than two feet;
Ahead, if I could descry anything,

Something, which seemed a thin, transparent sheet, $_{30}$

Held fort-like, proof against all entering.
Then I recalled my guide: where was he now?
Surely, ahead of me and if not following?

No going back, then, that at least I knew;
But anyway, my head could hardly turn,
So much I had but one path to pursue.

But how? What magic must my soul now learn?
I whispered in the faintness of this light,
'Dante, help me now: where is your strong arm?'

At first, mere void responded to my plight, $_{40}$
Some primal nothing as, perhaps, we think—
In error—buries us in its whole night,

But then, just when I felt my own soul sink
Within and hope about to be expunged
Forever, eyes saw, as on an ice rink

Where some consummate skater's fast, and lunged
Forward, behind we see markings in ice,
That spell a word engraved there as boots plunged,

Be it so brief, yet plain in their advice:
Which word brought me to tears, its letters were
 'Mercy'— $_{50}$
Like double sixes from unlikely dice

That reprimand against adversity

And where I was now; but more clarified:
Not boots but hands cut ice, and waved at me

As it were, beckoning beyond the dead
To join whoever these hands belonged to
And like him pierce the veil and forge ahead.

Mercy must mean, I reasoned, I must go;
That Power on high had given His assent
And—even as I thought—so I went through $_{60}$

As Mercy melt the veil and two hands lent
Assistance. There I was: the other side,
Collapsing, held by one Providence sent.

My mind all skewed, confused and hanging wide,
Aware the scorching heat and bitter cold
No longer burnt and froze my every side.

And I in someone's arms whose covering fold
Held me with a new strength whose depth spanned time
Deeper than Dante's did, if truth be told;

As if I needed more to make this climb $_{70}$
Than even Dante had in his reserves,
Infinite though they seemed compared to mine.

This blessing, then, more than I could deserve
Now infiltrated my soul with its touch,
Renewing purpose and upholding nerve.

I staggered back—straightening from my slouch

On those firm shoulders which had helped me through—
To see that one I felt I owed so much.

He stood four-square and somehow solid too,
Not like some ghost lain dead two thousand years. *80*
I can't explain but ... sure, his name I knew,

But couldn't say. Was it respect, or fear,
Or both? Between us then a moment's vacuum,
As I, from that grave face's deep austere,

Unable to turn or let my words come.
But then, he smiled. I blurted, 'Who are you?'
And 'Virgilius est nomen meum',

Immediately confirmed it was true:
The Roman poet who also knew hell;
Led Dante, like Dante, one of so few; *90*

Now here in what seemed an inverted bell
Of stone. Ahead—rising—a sheer rock face,
Behind—reversing—the merciful veil

That since re-formed to plug and block this place;
So going back nor forward neither seemed
Possible. Dante vanished, without trace.

I'd plumbed the depths, but had I simply dreamed?
That hospital, hallucinating on
My bed of torment with all those I'd named?

But Virgil beckoned me to come and join *100*

Him where he faced the wall, all resolute.
Ten cubits high, at least, its span,

And smooth as glass, no indent for a foot
To climb. No way—I saw—to gain its peak.
But Virgil turned; his hand seemingly alight,

He placed on that spot where I was so weak.
'The cancer has you here, and you must die,'
He said. 'So how will you find what you seek?

Know now: we enter where time comes alive,
Change cannot be stopped, everything decays, *110*
And you by sweat alone will not survive'.

He paused, as if deliberating ways
Of rescue. 'Still, all doors are open—for
That soul which yearns to believe, and so prays.'

Then, 'Tell me—what truly lies in your core?
Do you believe in One whose Hand can save?
Whose Hand can open even lockless doors?

Do you? Your state, as mine once was, is grave.'
I shuddered at his words, aching inside,
Especially at that point his touch moved— *120*

Stirring the fungal pottage to explode
And paste its spores throughout my living frame;
I hardly could hold in its intense load;

With it, too, came searing, unbearable pain.

'Virgil!' I cried. 'The cancer kills. Help me!'
But then I heard him mutter just one name:

'Phoebus Apollo! Now man—look up—see!'
Despite my suffering—which preoccupied—
New light flooded down, an outflow of glory.

I raised my eyes and there on top I spied $_{130}$
The god, magnificent, with bow and one
Arrow of silver forged in highest sky,

Whose flight accomplished what he willed be done.
So bright, his light obscured the pain I felt
And lifted my spirits, otherwise so down.

He raised his arrow, and as he did, knelt.
Then, in a move as fast as lightning strikes,
His arrow pierced the rock, which seemed to tilt

Till, suddenly, I heard, as thunder cracks,
Pure stone split, and the sheer face divide, $_{140}$
Twist, shift, as vein-like threads of plastered streaks

Recalling old age and its washed-up tide,
Appeared. What had seemed smooth was now upset—
Another cosmos with new rules applied.

Neither Virgil nor myself could stand or get
Our balance—wraith though he be—we both fell:
The roiling floor held us as in a net.

Perhaps endlessly stuck there, truth to tell,

Except at that moment Apollo's voice
Rang clear. 'You who have escaped deepest hell, *150*

Listen—to enter time is now your choice,
Proceeding further do, at your own peril,
Here change subtracts your pith and stills your joys.'

Ah! Desperate me, a-panic and feral:
Oracle clear—what greater warning of
Dangers ahead? But Virgil's mind held level.

'Now fix your mind and heart on Him above
And pray as Hezekiah prayed before.
Remember? Those ten steps that his God gave

When cancer all but had him dead for sure? *160*
Remember? Here are figs I will apply
As ointment to your wounds, to make them pure.

But pray.' So there I did immediately;
Yet, too, confused, for how could Virgil know
How God had saved that king destined to die?

However, of small moment that seemed so
As tumbling words, huge alphabets of sound,
Became alive and living streams of flow:

Great God! Reverbed, chorused all around
Till in the cavern of my very being *170*
Still God alone full occupied its ground

With waters in that instant's electric seeing:

For Hezekiah God brought the sun back
Ten steps; but I desired its forward bringing.

'Oh Lord!'—I cried—'By your great power, frack
These aging stones Apollo's seared with time;
Release your servants here where we are stuck—

Through your great purpose only, let us climb.'
At which words, silence, thick as cream gel
Clotted, ensued, as light flickered, grew dim: *180*

'Him Romans call Apollo, Uriel's
My name, the Cherub who guards the Garden Eden.'
This thunder-clapping speech broke through our spell

Which held us trapped below like denizens.
Now, where before his arrow cracked the stone,
He wrote with, directing its feathered end.

As he did so, each twist tore a fresh wound.
I wanted to cry out, and more, scream even,
Suffering beneath the god's ripping hand:

The price to pay were I to find real heaven. *190*
Beside me, almost I heard Virgil groan.
But how? But why? But then the rock was riven!

Slowly at first, like thread being unsewn—
Then wrenched open at not one but ten places,
Scaling entirely bottom to the crown

Where Uriel stood, his work unleashing spaces,

9

As now his face resumed its light. The pain
Brought me to fainting, even dying's crisis,

For I'd returned where change changes again—
All that that meant. Why Virgil too now hurt—*200*
Like Eurydice, as blood in her sweet veins

Began to start and run and jump and spurt,
To re-compose as near the entrance out,
So Orpheus saw her outline, at last sharp;

So sharp, so fine, so solid, without doubt ...
Then how his look unmade the soul he loved—
How pitiless the gods hearing his shout

Of agony—denied all he craved.
Now in reverse great Virgil became flesh
Again, could walk the path that led above.*210*

But greater wonders still awaited yet—
For Uriel's arrow had struck deeper far
Than anything I could imagine, guess:

Ten cracks of rock produced, each, their stone bar
Extruding, thus becoming level steps,
That to the summit proved an even stair.

Before us, only one cubit to leap
Where we could leave behind profoundest hell,
Ascend and not look back at that dark deep.

How Virgil studied his own hand—scanned well—*220*

Noticing every tremor of his blood,
Pulsing with life, and its resurgent swell.

Such his surprise at being done such good
In fascination stayed, as cobras do
When pungi players sway and fix their mood;

Oblivious to our nearby rescue,
So Virgil studied his re-forming arm.
I shouted, 'Lord, step up, we're nearly through!'

Though one past death might scarcely notice harm,
Suddenly Virgil acted with mastery:$_{230}$
He too had life and, with it, life's alarm!

Grabbing my collar—his first thought for me—
He whisked us up in one instant ascension
Where standing upright, ahead we could see:

What seemed a step was one massive extension—
Domain where frail spirits worked out their work
To find the truth beyond failed earthly visions.

I stood amazed: I'd surfaced like a cork
And as I did, I gulped the air relieved
To be beyond the sufferings of the dark.$_{240}$

Yet, too, it felt so odd because I lived
In this new clime so unlike that before.
But nothing this to what Virgil received:

He laughed, exulting from his deepest core;

Hands thrown up in holy hallelujahs,
Like David dancing with the ark, 'Lord, Lord!"

Unstoppable and unseemly chutzpah,
Almost. Condemn him I could not;
Instead, myself infected with new praise:

I sang aloud—'We have been saved by God'—$_{250}$
And as I did the whole domain beat time,
There dancing with Virgil, weaving new plots.

Perhaps to stay and sing and dance with him
Forever at that spot might not be wrong;
But urgency interrupted, broke in:

We were in time now and all its weird strange.
Our ecstasy subsiding, we aware
Slowly of one approaching from the fringe.

Virgil, his face all red where he'd perspired,
Now slackened to turn and greet this new-comer.$_{260}$
How leisurely time passed as we stood there.

Arriving, at last, and wonder of wonders,
Who was the more astonished, but God knows,
For who was the master and who the minder?

Both looked incredulous, as their eyes showed;
Both blurted out the other's name as one,
Together again, Providence allowed.

'Virgil,' said Dante, 'How can this be done?

I see you are yourself, Limbo behind,
Moreover, you have regained flesh and bone.$_{270}$

I live in heaven, and there see that Mind
Directly, which no-one comprehends
Except in glimmers so bright, glimmers blind;

But presence in Limbo is without end,
But here you are—' his words at this point failed,
Embracing Virgil, his dearest, once lost friend.

How Virgil choked, in his new flesh regaled,
Aware too much how roles had been reversed:
Dante no longer flesh, in spirit revealed;

But deeper still he knew just how the curse$_{280}$
Of Limbo had been broken, shattered even;
As adamantine by superior force—

Which done is obvious, a simple given,
But reckoning it's impossible before.
'You ask how I'm on this first step to heaven

When as a listless shade I left you where
Man's Paradise begins? Ah me! To tell
Now my true heart's restored within my core;

Now that I know—believe—makes my soul swell
Such as I am fit to burst and die again;$_{290}$
My eyes—' Long unfamiliar how to feel,

Burst into tears, as wrestling with his pain

Relieved, and gratitude beyond his sum,
Virgil attempted speech and to be plain.

Finally, 'Remember, the one who came?
Lady of Grace who left the Mother's side
To rescue one soul, Beatrice her name—'

At that naming, how Dante lit with pride,
Shone light—'she told me then that she would
Praise me often to Him, though I was dead; *300*

Before Him she always remained and stood:
Her favourite, ever before His Glory,
Before immortal power of her God,

Had time to waste, bibble-babble my story,
Her grace—'Again, he paused, as overcome
Through love, the fact that 'She had come for me

Too.' Virgil hung his head as if in shame,
Unworthy to share the joys that Dante had;
Yet through her, God had re-invoked his name.

Now Dante was like David dancing: mad! *310*
His joy could barely be contained, discerned
Within the range where human senses trade.

But, at last, stopping, to us both he turned
As new inspired: 'All things are through His Will,
And His Will and Presence cannot be spurned

Without destruction; which also fulfils

14

His plan, that puts time forward ten degrees
Which these steps show, and to climb is to heal.

God's added thirty years', he said to me;
To Virgil: 'At top of here a chapel rests₃₂₀
Where souls repair to find Luke's ministry.

When you are there, before His Cross that's blessed,
This Purgatory endured a second time
By you will yield its fruits and slough your flesh

To enter heaven—permitted by Him—
For yielding to God is this miracle—
The axle shifts; no longer pagan times

Are you accredited with, but One full
Of mercy, grace and that truth He revealed.'
We stood astounded, dummies doubly dulled,₃₃₀

As if his words had not inspired but killed.
Then Dante smiled—our prophet he'd become;
God's boundless goodness had been concealed

As life is, hidden in the hidden womb,
Until that birthing moment makes it plain
And what is really living issues, home.

Ahead, ten steps of steepest, stark incline;
But holding true, we rose to climb again.

CANTO 2: FAMILY

The Argument:

With Dante and Virgil, the poet now ascends the first stair, but before he can do so Virgil applies some much-needed medicine—the fig applied to Hezekiah's body long before. So revived, the poet reaches the stair where he finds to his utter astonishment someone he'd left behind long before in HellWard. The poet finds out their story and about the transformation that has been wrought and why. At the same time, under a covering shawl, another important character from the poet's past—who is in a dead trance—is being tended and consoled, unaware, but awaiting the day when the soul will arise and perfected souls can move up together.

On the first step I found myself with Virgil—
Dante; ahead a plain whose limit held
Some canopy shading a billion vigils

Where those of numberless origin told
Their tales—as a sweeping wave undulating
Might through its presence penetrate, enfold

All livingness in its constant vibrating;
A billion tuning forks in sorrow's key—
So beautiful the sound, and yet so grating,

Scraping regret inherent in all *Me*—10
That inescapable condition felt
Always, exhaling through the verb to be:

Here, seeing at last, what's truly our fault.
Within the melody I heard, so faint,
A note I knew, impossible and fraught.

Something I dreaded, but knew still could want.
I turned to Dante, who (wholly absorbed
Now with the Mantuan, clothed in flesh's paint)

Found matter witty, as they exchanged barbs
In Latin, and then Italian tongue;20
But I—wretch-like—took their happiness hard:

Surely, this hard-won place nowhere to lounge?
About to give them both a piece of mind,
When Dante turned—and what I would felt wrong:

For those eyes saw more than I'd understand
Ever. Ashamed, I bowed my head, aware
My mentor knew desires that had me bound.

He said nothing though, but simply stood there,
Awaiting how his teacher—articulate—
Would speak his words and spell us out from here. *30*

Imagine, reader, if you can, my state:
Two masters, companions knowing the way,
In them sure knowledge of deep dealing fate,

Yet in their midst there's time—it seems—to play
When all the while I hear the strain before
Demanding, whatever else, I not stray.

Then Virgil moved with all that skill of yore;
It seemed millennia only compounded
Strength in him, slow at first, but in his core:

And moving so, so spoke to my dumb-founded *40*
Condition; feeling where he rubbed the fig
Against the very spot where I was wounded;

Relief at last! His voice raised high, a fugue
Mixed in the rising tide of pain we heard,
So what was, sounded now another gig

Entirely: music more to be preferred,
As where rainfall is, the sun bursts through,
Or honey oozes where dead oak's interred;

Thus after thunder the wind gently soughs,
So pain lessened, as new hope multiplied— *50*
His other hand held high the golden bough.

And his words pierced me: 'I was one who died;
In Limbo knew—painless—the double death
Of those who cast the living God aside;

But see me now, living, lungs taking breath,
In flesh revived to go where I can't wait,
Because of her—the lady—prayed with faith

Before the face of Him who can create
From nothing worshippers, as I am one
Who rising thus—like my Lord—incarnate!' 60

As if to seal his words and what was done,
The step, in trampoline-like ecstasy,
Moved—seismic—joy another soul condoned;

And that through Him the dead, too, would un-die
Should intercession overwhelm that seat
Where the heart's prayer at last meets His fire's glory.

Amazed, and yet his words inspired my feet
To make one step forward, and then another,
Until, almost, myself a spirit, lithe and fleet,

Who's not held back by their own flesh, but rather 70
Propels itself just as intention wills.
Thus, from dallying, stuck in idle palaver,

All three of us felt the pull of the real
Ahead and calling—there we had to be
If, least, two destinies were to be fulfilled.

'This way,' I said. I knew, but could not see,
Much less explain how I could be so sure;
But both my masters didn't disagree.

There, westwards on this level, was a door;
Through it the source identified at first$_{80}$
Would be revealed—that perhaps—and much more.

A deep foreboding—something like a curse—
Began to weigh on me, as if above
Were truths more painful than Hell's depths might nurse.

'You are about,' said Dante, 'to find love;
Be not afraid—though pain's how it appears,
As you will find in what you do not have.'

His words then only amplified my fears;
So many questions I wanted to ask;
But now, before I could, through the shrill air$_{90}$

A holy wailing wrapped me in its cask;
So solid, pain was tangible—visible—
Peeling the skin as acid might a mask:

Wherein—I saw her—clawing for her soul,
Stripping away the layers plastered there
Through years, which now in shreds, plopped in the bowl

Beneath her bed, thin flakes signalling cure;
Repulsive to see flesh, and bleeding so,
Raw in its sore ugliness, and its scars;

But still below her surface lit a glow,*100*
As might a pumpkin on All-Hallows' Eve,
Horror outside, shaped in demonic woe,

Yet within not death now, at last to live.
For each flake of hers that fell, a tear too.
I watched her there and as I did I grieved

Inside my deepest heart; for she I knew,
Knew well, so well, who last I left for lost.
I tried to speak, but only silence grew.

Until, like magic, Dante's finger crossed
The air and on that summoning's sure sign,
My mother stopped, dumbstruck—as one accost—*110*

Then looked up. 'Son,' she said, 'Son, who is mine,
Forgive me now I know what pride I had;
Pride nothing could break ...only ... the divine...'

Her words trailed off, as no word known could add
One jot of sense to Whom she made allusion;
Howsoever empty all was, still is God;

That Word at least was true and no delusion.
As if confirming it, I heard him gasp
Behind, while Dante pushed me into motion:

Where no words speak, then its action we grasp.*120*
I fell before my mother in her shawl
And knew I too had forgiveness to ask,

But horror seized me, wanting to recoil,
From flesh she'd picked—still picked—flesh-like worm-
     holes
Of yellow matter or red like squished boils.

'I can't help it,' she sobbed, 'how I am foul;
But this—His mercy—shaped my penitence;
So digging within—I must find my soul.'

Thus she renewed her searching violence;
How gingerly, with fear, I reached my hand *130*
Out, touching, but as I did, my soul winced:

Her suffering, something I couldn't stand
To see, much less feel; but then contact made—
Across the sea, the mariner steps on land—

She paused—some tenderness perhaps allayed
The agony that proved her penance now;
But too the stench of flesh, rotting, decayed,

Suddenly changed, another scent in tow,
As lavender oil spilt from some huge vat
Might overwhelm dead ground where maggots grow. *140*

Its loveliness in just one second flat
Invaded all the air's stale whereabouts,
And light brighter than kindle brought to catch

Flared up—and its effects transformed her state.
'God wills I tell you how I escaped hell:
His mercies—too awful to contemplate—

But on them I am ever fixed and still.'
Around me—sensing Virgil, Dante, hushed
With expectation of my mother's tale—

All other thoughts and interests were crushed; *150*
For in her His mercy would be revealed.
'Dying, alone, with all my hopes ambushed

Because I had denied all God unveiled
Throughout my life, each opportunity
Let slip, in each real act of love, I'd failed;

Every thought had always been me, me!
The nurse came in to dress and I stood up;
Lying, as she left temporarily,

Suddenly removed—going, life's prop—
I coughed so gently, just two times, before *160*
The nurse worked out my heart, indeed, had stopped;

And while they fussed—the doctor through the door—
My spirit spun in spirals ever down
Through blackness in a blackened corridor.

In front, I saw a mouth in which I'd drown
Forever, mocking, always since my birth
Telling me: clumsy, ugly, and fly-blown.

To know inside myself: I lack all worth.'
At this narration stalled, but even so
The light beneath her harrowed skin surged forth *170*

And seemed to form a shape in its strong glow.
My mother murmured, 'Mother killed me then,
Intended it, from the first, long ago;

Two brothers dead, just children, never men;
And I to be the same, only four years
Old, hospitalised—saving me for ten.

Her mouth, a devil within it I swear:
Her words could kill—and oh! my soul—they did;
Through her I learnt my every worthless fear.

But mine is not to blame—see here what's hid.' *180*
With that one movement of her hand, so slight,
That shawl which covered her body just slid

Away, and there beneath, against her thigh,
Pressed hard, I saw him, as I had the last:
Unconscious, mumbling madly without light.

Her other hand held him there, held him fast
As if in tenderness to stroke his hair,
Comfort him for all they'd lost, all gone past.

'I called him 'Bastard', it's your father here;
He asked forgiveness as he lay dying *190*
And I refused—forgive!—refused to hear.

Now love compels, as long as he is lying
I am his comforter in his bleak hours;
For all I hated, love knows no denying.'

'Father!' I gasped, seeing him and aware
That no sound then could penetrate his cloud
Or make him wake—yet, as she stroked, some power

From somewhere deeper than deepest, allowed
Energy, breaking through his coma's still—
A twitch perhaps, flicker maybe aroused—$_{200}$

As if *enough* might drive out his dull evil,
Or Frankenstein's creature might come alive
But purged of folly and now pure in will.

And how her hand became a loving wife's
By practice in this long purgatory,
Became what most she needed, which was love.

Their marriage pointless and nugatory,
Except ... I saw existence everywhere
Contingent on such doings and, too, me.

The glowing light within now shaped a sphere,$_{210}$
Burning so brightly—such the hope she had—
Within I saw her soul's true face appear:

The one she'd lost, the one that had gone bad!
How beautiful now framed in that pure glow;
I saw—fleeting—how all creation's made

Whose secret, at root, only One can know!
Dazzled; but she resumed her tale to tell:
'I fell towards her mouth that would have swallowed

Me, keeping my soul forever in hell;
But just as mother's teeth, about to snap,$_{220}$
And I to be her victim perpetual,

Then, then—I heard with shock one thunder clap,
Which froze my fall—like space had no inch forward—
Like, better still, that time's second clock stopped;

A-trembling, what had held me going downwards?
There—with his beating wings, unbearably bright,
Angelic antidote to all the coward

In me. I could not stand to see his light
Or bear to contemplate the jaws ahead.
He touched my shoulder, effortless in flight;$_{230}$

And as he did I felt my hopeless needs
Evaporate. He said, simply, "Fear not—
Those prayers for you One knows and too is pleased."

As he said this, something undid—a knot
I'd had too long—and my soul, like some wick,
Just lit; and the cold-dead inside stirred hot;

And so, at last, a person I could like—
At least a bit—began to form within,
Which forming, made see me see my past sick.

I cried—my soul cried out only for Him,$_{240}$
But there the angel answered, took command.
'Now un-condemned, I have you, every limb;

That angel 'on your shoulder', now at hand,
So what you failed to learn's available—
Through level pain, you'll see the One, and stand.'

She paused. 'Pray James, for me, and pray in full—
Pray every time your eyes close, while you live;
Pray, knowing nothing deflects His searching will

That will not be gainsaid its harvest—love.
Inscrutable His majesty and power;
My heart yearns to suffer and be above250

With Him where, at last, He will tread the hours
To dust, and we will freely be like Him.'
Her speech astonished me—certain, assured,

And eloquent, as living she'd never seemed.
But Dante knew all this and simply glowed;
While Virgil expressed fresh hunger to climb

Immediately. I had to find the road—
The next level; but seeing her alone,
Except for tending my dead dad, she would

Comfort till time itself were one still stone,260
I could not move, or leave her in such state.
But she looked up then and her being shone;

Her hand stroked my father's head, her true mate,
Now tied to one whom she would never leave—
Two subjects, verbs destined to conjugate.

27

'I bless your going,' she said, 'so don't grieve.
Your journey's to eternal paradise;
But doing so, your route also will weave

Ways too I'll follow once this sacrifice
Is done.' She gazed, then, where her fingers stroked
His hair—as if there'd never been divorce: *270*

Every moment, movement, more pity evoked;
And seeing there my father's motionless head,
My past came back like food on which one choked.

The overwhelm!—I too needed a bed,
For I could hardly stand, But Virgil, firm,
I felt his arm and on his strength I fed.

Gasping for breath, absorbing all the harm
That had been done before, I teetered on
My feet, yet saw, in my mum's face, concern

For me. A smile flickered, and then was gone. *280*
The holes began to reappear she picked—
Much penance from her was still to be done.

Virgil held me, whilst Dante's speaking pricked
The hypnagogic bubble I'd been in:
'You have her blessing, James, at last you've clicked.

Now come—the levels above are widening;
If you're to climb the stairs and meet success
And reach the point of true awakening,

Then understand so little time is left.
Your mother nearly lost it all at death.
She bids you now, while you are in your flesh, *290*

For her sake reach the summit and unleash
That mercy which alone may draw her up.'
He paused. 'Your father too is my belief.'

His words filled me with hope, powerful and apt.
I knew that looking back was a mistake,
So let great Virgil, his arm round me wrapped,

Guide me forward to find another place
Where we'd ascend the stairs to healing's space.

CANTO 3: EX-WIFE

The Argument:

Reluctantly, the poet has left his mother behind nursing his father, as she awaits her transformation through belated devotion to him. Dante explains how it is possible for the poet's mother to be in HellWard and yet on the StairWell. They encounter the wall of ice and Dante saves the poet and Virgil. From this step they come upon the sands of gold where Midas reigns and his queen: the poet's ex-wife! She tries to turn him into a block of solid gold, but revealing a lost secret stymies her efforts and a remarkable butterfly sets off on its incredible journey ahead of the poet.

No looking back as forward we stepped forth
To find the spot where we'd escape this level—
Its melancholic dirge, lack of self-worth,

And self-absorption leading to its evils—

Though left in better hope and light aspiring.
Yet in my mind some irritant or cavil

Still rankled like burnt-out wood that's still firing
Sparks in a blackness where the soul is stretched:
Something did not make sense, something terrifying.

I had this double vision burnt or etched $_{10}$
Into my head as might a cattle brand
There be imprinted; so visibly pitched

That Dante, always my friend, took my hand
To guide me into truth. 'You wonder late—
For leave we must your mother in this land—

How you have seen, in this more hopeful state
Who gave you birth; and yet also below
Where those persist who cannot change their fate?

How can this be? Has fate been struck a blow?
Has God no longer got control, and more: $_{20}$
Has Typhon unleashed full chaos in tow?

In Hell you were with her, and now she's here.'
He paused, allowing his words their effects,
The which exactly mirrored all my fears.

I yearned within to know heaven's true text.
So he began: 'Remember great Odysseus?
How with sublime terror beyond the Styx

He summoned one hero, greatest of us,

Greater than himself—baldric made of gold—
There hell-bound, Herakles, son of Zeus; *30*

But Homer notes another truth be told:
That hero-phantom's there, but the real man's
Above with deathless gods in their stronghold.

So you have seen your mother's eidolon—
Her husk stripped off from whom she truly is,
Like some memorial that wasn't planned;

How late your prayers' potent efficacies
(Were laid and willed before the world was made)
Transport your mother finally to bliss.'

I stood stunned: this gift, an unworldly trade, *40*
That One above whose mercy knows no measure,
Released her because—and I wept—I prayed.

'Your words,' I said through sobbing, 'give me pleasure,
But too, as we approach the higher stair,
Get nearer still to Him; and I, a creature,

Worm-like, unworthy, feel dread, awe and fear
As by electricity shocked and charged.
To flee His presence's best and not be here!'

I turned determined where I'd lately urged
To go not so to do. And Dante's hold *50*
Failed in its grip; but solid Virgil lunged

Before my path, assertive, blocking, bold

And countermanding. 'I am proof', he said,
'Only above's where you'll find your true world;

No fear must lead you back to Limbo's bed,
There idly lounging in its timeless waste
Or worse. I know—think you I don't know dread?

For even now, though flesh-riven, re-cast,
Recalled to higher purpose by her prayers,
I tremble so my inner being's aghast. ₆₀

A pagan, I, and now to stand before
The Lord of lords, the God of gods, the One?
Yes, barely—or not conceive what's in store

As rising we ensure destiny's done?'
Then, touching me his hand, human and warm,
Spirit within and shadow still strapped on—

Unlike Dante through whom light like bees swarmed—
I felt release and knew I had to rise.
'Forgive me,' I cried, 'My courage less firm

Than yours; but now I see, and in your eyes ₇₀
I find that fire which led the Trojan from
Ruins below to highs of Roman glories.'

And as I spoke those words, so then we came
Abruptly where the stair now formed a wall,
Or barrier ending advance on this platform.

Behind us, millions moaning in their dull

Lament, which I for sure wanted to leave.
Some nine or ten feet up—so how to scale?—

And smooth as ice, which to touch was to freeze:
It glistened in its lonely corner slot; *80*
Inviting, though only to those naïve

Enough to think they could escape their lot
Without paying the full indemnity
Their case demanded; no-one reached the top!

I feared the ice: how it would affect me,
So loath, therefore, even to touch its sheen;
But Dante knew the way to protect me:

Bid Virgil beside the far corner lean
Just off, his hands cupped tight, bid me step up—
With him to push and me to jump the plain. *90*

Nothing for it but boldness, so I leapt—
To find myself alone, and they beneath.
I would have turned, but found my viewing stuck

On what ahead amazed and took my breath:
It seemed I stood where all the ground was gold,
Small particles of it, stretching in breadth

From where I balanced at the ledge's fold.
Like ice crystals at the point where I poised,
But shifting in colour from the silvery cold

I'd left for yellow's warm and deep, deep glaze. *100*

As on a peak, wondering with fond surmise,
Riches enough to last for endless days,

Merely by scanning ground, playing I-spy!
So, transfixed was I, until his voice broke—
And he there beside me—my reverie.

I nearly fell back—how had he...? —the shock—
But his hand grasped me firm—I did not fall,
But realised through this I must awake.

I wanted then most to confess it all:
The hunger, seeing gold in such abundance; *110*
But something else needed instant recall:

For where was Virgil, left behind long since?
My appetite had so deranged my mind,
So much had gold re-made me to lose sense.

Sheepish, as one in a field left behind
Who suddenly aware feeling exposed,
Trots quickly to catch up, hoping to find

His flock. I turned—below the master paced
In evident irritation—my fault.
'Mercy, my lord,' I cried. 'Here, I'm well-placed'. *120*

With that, I leant and stretched my hand, and caught
His own; with all my strength I strained to lift
Him, and did so, but as his feet pushed taut

Against the ice's wall to give legs' shift,

Clenched hands instantly suffered a cold charge
Strong as an arctic storm's paralysing drift.

I wanted to let go—so my blood urged,
But neither I nor Virgil now could do.
I saw his teeth chatter, and his face purge

Of live colour, draining to a sick blue. *130*
My own like-wise the same: both doomed
To face each other, held by cold's fast glue,

Forever. Even thinking stopped, it seemed,
For I could not muster thought to shout
Aloud for help—only within, I screamed.

Another minute and, surely, no doubt
We'd be conjoined in form no better than
That which Medusa's frozen stare induced:

Mere relics of humanity, not men—
What point to have left Limbo far below, *140*
Or written epics, struggling with the pen—

To come thus far, and yet no more to go?
What was it here that I could never face?
Or secret God might never let me know?

But as I lay benumbed, prostrate and dazed,
Above me, something like the thinnest sound
Shuffled, or whistled in its own way crazed.

I felt it—hand stab my back, dealing its wound—

An expert martial artist who breaks bricks—
Whose hand cuts in to grasp the heart it finds, *150*

Still living, just. The pain! I retched up sick,
But as I did the fiery heat he had
In that hand burned with undiminished wick,

Kick-starting life, the movement of my blood,
And through my fingers Virgil too revived.
One jump, he made it up. We'd done it. Good.

But his hand who'd struck me, and compromised
My body, now I saw as in slowed motion
Returning, like swarming bees to their hive,

Where silence, after all their agitation, *160*
Resumed its shape as Dante's hand turned hard—
My glimpsing spiritual operation.

I needn't ask—I knew without a word
How he'd appeared beside me at the ledge,
So longed to be like him, which longing spurred

Me on. I stood, then, all ready to budge
And move forward, but Dante—preoccupied—
As one who senses danger on a bridge

Stands still—though what could trouble one who'd died
Already? Virgil's welfare, or my own? *170*
Being in flesh, aware of our weak side;

The ice had almost caught us, cast us down:

Too credulous, too rash by far we were;
And now ahead—not green—a pure gold lawn,

Except perhaps more like a wetland mere
The sun's rays strike and bounce back from, to blind
Our eyes, irradiate the atmosphere;

Exciting or what? A-shimmer the mind
Caught with desire to throw oneself into
That gold that so beguiled. 'Beware this pond *180*

Of particles so fine; who'd think or know
This ocean's deeper far than steps can sound?
And many are—mis-stepping—sunk below.

See, clear your vision, ears un-wax, unwind
From worldly threads that you may pass harmless
Here.' Dante's words seemed ominous, profound;

We paused, uncertain, and I most seeming gormless;
But Virgil took first sight: 'I see strange shapes,
Attracting as they shift to form from formless.'

'Still wait,' said Dante, 'only here is hope; *190*
Illusion beckons each one to their doom;
Pray, too, He strengthens you, that you will cope.'

At just that point, one form closed in, a dome
Which berthed beside us, like a moving island
That we might step on—and enter its room.

We did. And there she was. 'Hello my husband,'

38

She said, and I almost convulsed with shock.
Now, if ever, time to quit this fool's errand!

'I can't,' I mumbled, staggered, 'what the fuck?'
But Virgil held me up, he understood. *200*
'James, for you there can be no going back;

The tears of things are in your flesh and blood,
As you will find.' I stood there paralysed,
Within conflicted—feelings stuck in mud.

There, burnished with gold that her soul so prized,
The chair she sat on; and beside the gifts
That we'd exchanged in love, but she had seized.

Two rings, a bracelet—pure gold—other thefts
Of lesser value, and there the amulet,
Centre of all, which left me most bereft: *210*

Gold chain, with coffin figure, within set
Ivory inlaid to fill its key-like core;
Recalled to me what I'd tried to forget,

I turned to Dante, if he could help more?
Impassive, though, he stared straight through the queen,
Seated, quite unaware his presence there;

And Virgil—well—to him, what did it mean?
'I rule here,' she said. 'And here my writ runs,
For Midas grants me power which nothing screens:

One touch of mine is deadlier than a gun; *210*

Flesh even turns to what I want, more gold!
Why—' Here she stood. 'Once James, we two were fun;

But look now—you are poor, ha! You are old!
So let me touch, and ease your misery;
Your value I'll increase one hundred-fold!'

With that—her ominous first step towards me—
I tensed, treading backwards, in total fear,
My wretched mind revolving desperately—

Like some wasp buzzing in a locked jam jar,
Below it, perilous waters waiting patient—$_{220}$
And all I did not want looming so near.

The StairWell proving some deceptive agent
Delivering back to the Hell I had escaped
But lately. Indeed, some abortifacient—

For if I failed now, what would be my state?
Distracted by impending doom, I turned—
Only to see the white ivory inlaid

Within the amulet, as in an urn,
Sacred, devoted, as some congealed ash
No fire destroyed, though thoroughly it burned.$_{230}$

Her hand reached out and with its merest brush
I too would be a brute inanimate,
And all my hopes for heaven helpless, crushed.

But in that space where time itself lacks state,

As neither forward nor backwards to go,
A knife-edge either way deciding fate,

So there I was, the amulet a-glow,
For why? What secret did ivory own—
Somehow to continue I had to know.

'Hari,' I blurted, 'ivory's real bone:₂₄₀
That child we had together, you destroyed,
His flesh and blood consumed, and his soul's gone

To heaven!' I cried to God. "My dear boy!'
No more her peril vexed me or her touch—
Something had been lost money couldn't buy,

Or all the gold she'd stored in her greed's pouch.
And she—as ivory preoccupied
My mind—too felt its memory, and blanched,

Stalled in her tracks—remembered her boy, dead;
One she'd forced down and out her crotch's chute.
'I don't care, I don't care,' she said, and lied.₂₅₀

For now, some tear—but one as black as soot—
Tried forming in the corner of her eye,
But finding release from her flesh, could not.

Held back, held onto, so how could she cry?
Where was release? Within, a speck before
Not visible, now half-crawled out, a fly

Lodged on her duct, so well fed, dripping spores,

Bloated, and like its mistress, simply stuck
There: far too fat to leave, effect a cure.

And yet, half out this way, wriggling—a crack$_{260}$
Appeared in her countenance, as askew
Eye saw the fly and memory brought back

The clinic—killing—and the wrong she knew
She'd done—dead child of whom I only dream,
How in my heart my being longs for you!

Yet, yet ... she took your life before your name
Was ever called—who are you? And what be?
See us—me too—this golden waste of shame

Around—deserts of her idolatry!
But she, constricted, choked and rendered dumb,$_{270}$
Could hardly move, much less attack, touch me.

That fatal moment when God's judgement comes,
Which every human gets to at some point,
Deciding whether they go up, slip down,

And now, her eye blotted as by black paint,
Disfigured as its fly expanded forth,
She turned, staggered as one about to faint,

But holding up until she felt support—
Grasping the amulet—pressing in my hand—
Rendering back to me our dead child's worth$_{280}$

In ivory. And as she did I understood

Or thought I did—she now hysterical,
Yet silent as a block of hardest wood

For nothing could come out, compressed withal;
We both may, shocked, have stayed there till doom's day;
But short steps to the edge, that was all,

As Dante herded, bid us not delay;
The desert-ocean had its golden shore,
A precipice on which last outcomes played.

But what she did next, why, I wasn't sure:$_{290}$
Collapsing down as Crassus did, his throat
To be the moat on which the Parthians poured

Gold loved so much by him. Another note,
However, sounded as of some release:
A flapping, light, as if about to float,

And not that hostile buzzing of disease
Infecting her eye; I looked, and there, red
Which black before, was struggling but to seize

Its living back, which for so long had fled;
So now in metamorphosis red changed,$_{300}$
First black to red and then even that bled

Away. At last, all had to be expunged.
Around my knees she clung, began to wail,
Her very eyes—liquefying squeezed sponges—

If that her tears so long held in her soul

Might finally be free—but fluttering,
I saw it, heard a new voice say it all:

The fly—no longer one—now took to wing,
A butterfly so beautiful, so light,
So graceful, its sight induced in me song—*310*

Charged and transported—I'd made paradise,
At least in that moment. I wondered hard
To see it soar so fragile, free in flight,

But more still—a wonder I preferred:
Below, gold altered so, its dust to brown
With shoots of green, as if the conscience stirred

Meant earth returned, reclaimed its own,
And what was dead might incredibly live
Through Him whose dying, death couldn't keep down.

Quiet, she stood beside me now. 'Forgive,'*320*
At last, she said, and what else could I do?
'With all my heart,' I said, 'But I must leave.'

But now beside us, stood Dante, Virgil too,
Standing as if awaiting some last act
Which I'd commission though what, I didn't know.

Ahead, the ground her butterfly had raked
With aerial beauty, now seemed fertile soil,
Living and moist, half solid and half lake.

My palm felt warm: in it, about to sail,

I felt the amulet expanding fast ₃₃₀
Eager to launch and be free of its gaol.

I knew then what to do: one motion cast
The gold away and ivory in it.
See, how it flashed in flight, and fell at last

Into the lake-land's alive, living pit,
Wherein, not sinking, but like a small boat
Held up, and following—with innate wit—

Her butterfly on its long, distant float.
How tiny—ivory in such a big sea,
But even so it seemed bigger, full of hope: ₃₄₀

Indeed, as I strained my eyes, tried to see
More, yes, becoming clear, expanding, there
The gold dissolving, but not ivory—

I saw its shape take form, taking in air,
Enlarging as if new breathing began—
And in my heart of hearts I found a prayer,

A blessing: I was seeing my lost son—
Whom she had killed—adrift, and in pursuit
Of where his mother's butterfly would land.

I waved—like some lost soul's desperate salute; ₃₅₀
Perhaps his eyes were formed and he'd respond—
Or lips cry, 'Father'! But his lips were mute.

As slowly the ivory confined went beyond

My vision, I felt my being shut down,
Go quiet, struggling so to understand—

My breath to hardly breathe, or heart to pound.
Yet all the while, as sight became a speck
On the cruel world's vast and receding round,

I saw the body form: its head from neck,
Limbs shaping outwards in perfect legs, arms; 360
I sensed his blood even, suffuse his cheeks;

And as I did my inner self went calm.
I turned, full knowing I'd not see again
My precious boy; yet now what was, was balm.

Heroic child, though you were never born—
Like Herakles to the furthest western point
To find Hesperides, fearless you'd gone;

Over the horizon's edge, the while each joint
Of you reformed itself into the one
I call, 'My son'. You did not disappoint. 370

She stood there, still crying, tears still not done;
Till Dante touched her shoulder—so light, deft,
I'm sure she barely felt; but change came on,

As nakedness is altered once it's dressed,
As if the honey of his hands allowed
Her emptiness to have some sweetness left.

'Hari,' I said, 'You've cried. I too broke vows;

And now our boy flies to the Western Isles
Whom we may never see just once—God knows—

His living eyes. So let us—without guile—*380*
Forgive—commit to love our other child;
At last, then—' here I choked—'end this turmoil:

Conclude today what our mad years made wild.'
She stood, she looked for all the world as lost,
Drained—majesty void, divested, and grown old;

Who'd think to grow so rich might end a cost?
Had even Dante's touch restored her soul?
I sensed beside me Virgil anxious most

To move on—we could not let Hari stall
Our progress: other levels beckoned near,*390*
Already time ran out. I felt the pull

Ahead. 'Hari, listen—we've lost what's dear—
Almost ourselves as well in what we did;
I must go, climb further and leave you here,

But you must not permit your pain be hid,
Returning to those sterile, golden shores,
Pretending Midas can be your true god.

Your butterfly's exposed that god's lush flaws;
Gird yourself, and prepare to follow him
When grieving's done and ego's emptied, poor.*400*

She stirred then—tremulous—a sort of whimper.

Finally, 'Why bring me out of the womb?
Why not be dead before I have a name?

Why live where I can never be at home?
Why knees receive me and why breasts to nurse?
Why not in darkness stay than living roam?

Perish the day my father blessed my birth
And said, 'O joy—to us a daughter's born.
No, rather, begetting, let him be cursed.'

With that she stopped, and teetered over, swooned. *410*
I caught her just in time. With Virgil's help
We laid her where fresh lilies lately grown

Adorned a bank of solid earth, not pelf,
All that was gone—a new world dawned; and she—
A beauty sleeping there—might come to health

Once some angelic prince—but never me—
Arrived and with one kiss her soul would start.
But we'd no time to dither, destiny

Must run its course. To see her broke my heart
Thus on the ground. But Dante urged the way *420*
Before, and going meant we'd shed the hurt.

So, one last time, I knelt just where she laid
And gently kissed her forehead, and said, 'Bless.'
At last, some sort of peace between us made.

Not looking back, but that last tenderness

I treasured in my soul and more beside:
Where had he flown—my son—I could not guess?

Onward, both Dante, Virgil with huge strides
Pressed forward, as if leaving me behind,
So dilatory I, and now the gulf so wide;*430*

I ran as one possessed, or out of mind,
To catch them up, when round a sudden bend
They disappeared, so ominous a sign:

To lose my mentors and come to this end—
How would I fare without their wisdom, love?
I raced with all the strength I had to mend

How far apart we were—and reached the curve
Where they'd gone round but, as I did, stopped short,
Amazed—before my eyes, rising above

The whole landscape, stood a bridge, metal, taut,*440*
All shiny, surface smooth as polished steel—
Far side a building, political, fraught

With all of thinking's miscegenated ills:
A school, to wit, where education deals.

CANTO 4: PEER

The Argument:

The poet ascends the third stair where he finds a futur-
istic vision, built through education and Pelagian beliefs.
A huge complex constructed through advanced technology awaits
him. But there he meets an old business colleague that he now
barely recognises. Friendly in the extreme, he invites the poet,
Virgil, and Dante within. All is not what it seems, however, until
Dante exposes what the poet's old colleague, called Ness, really is.
Despite that, the poet falls into a copper trap, though is rescued by
Dante. Ness dramatically seeks to preserve his kingdom through
force. His poison arrow, though, backfires and the poet finds
himself inspired to save him.

How bright the future seems from where one stands
Stuck in a present where light most seems dim;
How little faith we have in now—beyond

Is better, always there where we must climb.
The architecture, flash metals and cords
Of twisted wire suspend—like massive limbs

Heaving their own trunk upwards—a huge high road
That purposes drive-throughs to paradise;
And mechanised, each person takes his load—

No load so heavy, vile, vicious—such vice!—*10*
As is turned back at some dullard's toll-booth
Where easy's their game, minute their excise.

I stood there, then, stupefied by such truth:
This brave new world which human beings built
From where I was seemed towering and aloof;

Though on the near side, close, two figures knelt.
Instantly I knew who they were and breathed
Relief: my masters—whose love I couldn't fault.

But why crouched so? To study strange beliefs
Half-hidden by the metal's overlay,*20*
Which, covering earth, helped hide its deepest grief?

As I approached, my Dante turned to say:
'Timely, my son, you come to see this rot—
See here—who'd think this structure (strong to stay)

Might through the slightest wind fall into Not?
All this is sweet philosophy awry;
From human minds whose principles forgot

The first. We go and soon will see just why
Every civilisation mankind's made,
No matter how glorious or how high, _30_

Descends from high vision to paltry trade,
And last becomes a racket and a cheat
Through which its own citizens dig their grave.'

I looked just where the earth on metal ate
Its root—and where the dingy rust, like red
Slime, penetrated its once pristine state.

Forebodings, I felt, of what lay ahead,
As something Preference would like not to see:
All dreams of mankind in ruins, quite dead,

A litter of carnage—called history— _40_
Which cut down to size all the vaunting up;
But I too was human, this too was me!

Here Virgil helped, for he knew empire's map
More than most; had stood beside Octavian
When all war's fortunes fell in his lap;

Had known supreme the power over land,
As well control of Homer's wine dark seas;
What it meant possessing total command

And its illusions—preaching Roman peace,
The while subjecting the whole middle Earth _50_
To violence, slavery, orgiastic feasts.

'I praise the One I died before His birth
In Palestine; Tiberius had no hold
Of me, and I no part to laud his worth

In poetry. For Caesar, Pilate failed
The basic test: not justice even, but
Their own—the law—served up both cold and spoiled.

Great futures, once so open, now all shut.
Be strong in faith; remember my lost plight—
Deader than ancient Rome, in Limbo; yet $_{60}$

Despite no hope of ever seeing light,
She who is lovely beyond words, or what
Words mean or could, made my name burnish bright

Before the Throne—her mercy burning hot—
Enkindling His creative flame anew
To change direction and rescue my lot.

Such is His mercy—what mercy must do;
Yet who predicts whom mercy will uphold?
Naked I was, but now enclothed to view

In flesh, so that my spirit in fresh mould $_{70}$
Might make this journey upwards, and with you.'
He ceased, but his words—like honey—had healed;

Himself foremost, but 'with you' meant 'we two'.
Before God's grace, no ranking, all was grace;
My own poor verse had its purpose also;

And Virgil—friend—I knew now face to face.
With Dante, then, together we stepped upon
The great metallic arch to this new place,

And daylight grew in the sky—still more shone—
So that I felt renewal and ascent,
For mercy meant that there was hope for man. 80

We reached the midpoint; from there the bridge bent
Downwards to end in buildings—as complex
As fuses in a box, charged with intent.

I saw some enter where a door said 'Lex'
And then in smaller letters, 'Welcome to
This bright new age of gender, not of sex;

Be as you want, be as you choose to do;
Learn freedom here from beings being equal.'
Cryptic to say the least, but Dante knew,

Saw through what this was, what would be its sequel. 90
'They think they mean well,' he said, 'and know best;
But ever agitating, never tranquil,

Until the world's perfect, they can never rest;
One mind, one technology at a time,
Like Tubal-Cain, ingenious, but not blessed;

All works secular and despite God's sign;
This ends—' Before he finished a voice called,
'James!' There he stood, was beckoning me in.

I knew the face, the voice, but his gait fooled
Me, as we marched towards the open door $_{100}$
Where welcome stretched out his hand and pulled

Us all within—so we'd see what he saw.
I scarcely knew what dumbfounded me most:
The architecture and what it was for,

Or who he was, his memory almost lost,
But on the tip of my tongue, and the shame
That comes forgetting one who is our host.

'Please introduce me, James; your friends have names?
Then let me take you all—for no-one's left
Behind—to view in grand immortal frames $_{110}$

And ever higher siliconic cliffs,
The future.' There he paused, smiled benignly,
As one who never knew conditional 'ifs'.

I looked again, wanting to be kindly,
But then I noticed what seemed curious, odd—
Each way I looked, always he turned to me;

Always I stood looking straight at his body;
For Virgil too, the same; and only Dante
Viewed his perspective from a different mode.

We, flesh-bound, saw what Ness—his name!—wanted; $_{120}$
However, Dante's spirit saw far more—
While I presented, Dante subtly planted

Himself beside a wall—one sheet of mirror—
Polished perfect with its futuristic sheen,
But that did not conceal the present here:

Virgil's eyes, mine too, shifted to his scene:
Ness, face-on, regular, good-looking guy,
But from the glass we saw his horse's mane,

Two hooves, long belly, strong flanking thighs.
Friend Ness a centaur! One, though, in denial *130*
Certainly, using some technology,

Appearing straight ahead in every portrayal;
For some reason seeming, not being straight,
Which caused me doubt—was he really so genial?

But as I wondered, I'd not long to wait:
Clearly impressed, though not by me, but by
Those reputations even he must rate—

Dante and Virgil—above him, so high,
But then again so wrong, for after all
They'd no technology with which to fly;

So time to show his rise, their future fall; *140*
How literature itself could not compare
With that adaptable machine his will—

Not Muse—created; and so we were there—
In an instant transported to his special room,
Dazed. Here, we learnt his god's real name: the Future.

Millions—uncountable—mingled in the gloom
Of that bright and sparkling vision he had—
He gave them life, but they all seemed like drones

Persisting through the drudge technology made;
How small the world appeared, how deadening, dull; *150*
I could not make out anyone's true trade

Or gifts, as each adapted to the cells
And screens electronically yanking their minds;
Not one had strength to turn, resist its pull.

'Light TRISH,' he said, and suddenly, like blinds
Removed, the room's opaque became a glare
Of cold and frigid light, and from behind,

As from a hidden safe, a jacket—rare
And made of copper plates, all glossy glitz,
Each one so small, heavy—hardly to wear— *160*

Appeared. 'For you, James, and I know it fits.'
I sensed that Dante disapproved, but why?
Me fool whom trinkets serve to lose my wits,

I took it from his hook, so hopefully
At first, and put it on. And while I did,
Ness chattered on, 'Pelagius, you know, really

Takes credit here—he made the future wide
Open for mankind, resisting the church,
Its stranglehold and anti-progressive side.

Heaven isn't gained by faith, but by work. *170*
I'm building heaven here, and you can join.'
Tongue-tied myself—beside me Dante lurched

Forward—whilst some dark charge throughout my loins
Rendered my senses stricken what to do.
But then I heard the mighty Dante stun

With words of magic—or poetry—all true.
'You prophet of heaven, profit's what you want—
Now turn and see the beast that's really you!'

Ness froze—not much a beast then, more still-plant;
Did pointing out his flanks, engender doubt?
Would he, through Dante's power, soon be shent? *180*

As beasts who in the air uplift their snouts
Sensing a danger, now—and how so!—quickly—
Ness grabbed a quiver off the wall to shoot

At Dante. Pretending sorrow, 'Sorry,
But you must not prevent my future plan,'
He said. 'Your views are retrograde and sickly.'

With that he loosed the bow straight at the man
(Forgetting how celestial beings are
Immune to all the worst flesh ever can

Do). Yet for all his total miscued error, *190*
Direct and into Dante struck the tip
Of his dire-toxic, Hydra-poisoned arrow

And veered through—swerving off, as if it slipped—
Could not connect with that immortal substance
Now Dante is; so passing gave it fillip,

As now not slower, still faster its advance,
Till striking me with full and fatal force,
Just at the point my heart pulses—no chance!

I would, should, have died instantly, of course;
But I'd put on the copper coat—I gasped: $_{200}$
The blow went home, dented, but did not pierce—

Electrics blown, my soul released, unclasped,
Uncoupled from the power the copper had;
The while the arrow bounced, and newly tasked

Whizzed back to see itself—mirror ahead.
Alarmed, Ness turned and, double-visioned, saw
His own true self and where its pathway led.

Too late to step aside, avoid its score:
The arrow bounced back to blight his right eye,
Blinding, whilst delving deeper in his core. $_{210}$

Still I hear it—haunting—his helpless cry,
Collapsed in agony, wailing one word, TRISH!
Shirt bloody, blood splashing technology,

Which could not save him now or grant his wish.
He struggled, writhed and screamed upon the floor—
'The cure, TRISH, the cure—your analysis?'

Mechanical, as algorithmic spores
Which multiply answers in secret cells,
So TRISH computed, then computed more:

'The Hydra's poison—there's no cure at all. $_{220}$
Your death is imminent. Shall I shut-down?
Your future is not yours. Who takes control?'

From writhing pain—her words—Ness turned to stone,
Realisation come so sudden—hard—
An analgesic, temporary, for his pain.

But in the lull, before his death's reward,
His one good eye lit up, reason returned:
He croaked, 'James, help me—you know I'm a fraud—

I see it now, though blinded, true goodness I've scorned;
Now help me, I'm dying, dying to hell.' $_{230}$
I stood amazed—his plea—and plight that formed

So clearly, yet so difficult to tell:
For Dante's way led up, but now I'd found
That even backwards routes go down StairWell.

Awkwardly stooping, joining on the ground,
I touched with tenderness around his head
And close as I could get nearest his wound,

Aware its poison's touch, and I'd be dead.
He sighed—to feel my touch and know I cared?
'Dear Ness, forgive my carelessness,' I said; $_{240}$

Truly, so lost, the while that I'd been spared,
Such guilt sprang up in me, and how surprised
I was so far from hell and still not cured—

Indulgence? Puss and gore in Ness's eye
Yet my own soul was what I thought about;
Worse still—beside one lost in purgatory.

'The lights, the lights!' he wheezed, 'are going out:
My other eye grows dim, my head feels numb!
My certainties are turning into doubts.'

That word—'doubt'—triggered in me love for him, _250_
For who had ever seen the One not seen?
The One who stretched out space and started time?

The One whose Spirit moved the hearts of men?
One hand of mine reached Ness's heart, the other
Held his, and as it did I prayed again:

An image formed and I whispered 'My brother!'
I heard TRISH glitch as if her code went wrong;
I heard above the shattering of rafters

And metal screech in its own razor-tongue;
How long could even the future's house stand? _260_
'Now Ness, recall, believe, the Lord is strong—

No devil's wit, or Hydra's bile's beyond
His reach or power to subdue all things.'
I thought of where I'd been and all the damned

I'd faced, yet here remained as lax as string
Unstretched: forceless, him dying, what to do?
What wisdom Dante or Virgil might bring ...

I nearly turned to ask. But then a clue
Appeared that I could not, would not accept:
From out his right eye a clot of poisoned glue $_{270}$

That issued ugly in its burning hex;
But from his left, just as his gargling throat
Gave breath whose last indeed would be his next,

I saw one long and lacerating tear float
Forward and down his sad and pallid cheek,
And I was called—by grace—to change its route.

How easy to turn, with masters to speak,
Deciding this and that the while life speeds
Its way. But now—this?—is not what I seek!

But moments only left—not words but deeds— $_{280}$
Inspired by Him who only is true wise—
My finger lifted, dipped in the bead-

Like tear still hanging, and wiped from his eye;
Trembling with fear, fear strong to floor an ox,
I knew my life surely a sacrifice.

That one tear on my finger's end, I flexed,
And like some painter—artist—with a brush,
His tear together with that vile glue mixed.

Touching the poison, immediately a rush
Shot up my arm, so that I thought my death $_{290}$
Certain—I almost felt that was my wish.

Instead, the rush—beyond my elbow—left,
Like some gale threatening, never reaching land,
Blown out. And Ness, a sudden gasp of breath,

But I looked, looked and could not understand:
There, in his eye, tear on that oozing mass
Of septic matter something came to mind.

At first not clear, I peered to see what was:
A blood-red tint infused, as in a pearl,
A shape forming exactly like a cross— $_{300}$

'And there—there—there'—I screamed! No pearl—the
      world
The cross superimposed upon. 'It's Him!
I've seen the One!' Around me Virgil kneeled

And Dante sang, as Ness stirred into time;
Myself collapsed, awe-filled and over-brimmed.

CANTO 5 MENTOR-BOSS

T
he Argument:

Overwhelmed by the vision of the One, the poet is carried by Virgil, whilst Ness is lifted high by Dante, as they continue their ascent. Arriving at a fourth and decrepit step where modern education takes place, Virgil asks the poet what he saw and to try to describe it almost induces another trance. But then they encounter the Head of Education, Kier, the poet's old boss and mentor, now in a pitiful state and, indeed, a state related to Ness. Yet, through grace, Kier praises the poet's teaching skills and via Dante then feels his connection with Ness. As Kier works to revive Ness an incredible and astrological transformation takes place and the Earth shakes. Their purpose to climb is renewed.

> I heard such humming, not mumbling of words—
> Language sounding, but in another key;
> Perhaps as that exchanged between sweet birds,

Or that noise shared in hives of honeybees,
Beyond the reach or span of mortal ken—
Below the threshold of humanity

Sustaining burdens—all that's ever been.
Did Dante sing? I now—potato-sacked—
Whom Virgil carried on his shoulder's beam,

So strong with all the flesh his soul now packed; $_{10}$
And I saw too how Dante lifted high,
As effortless, the centaur Ness, still sick

From his near death, still destined to die
Unless it be he'd find another cure.
How strange it was, ascending to the sky

But footless myself, with Virgil so sure.
The viaduct we travelled seemed so short,
Easy compared to that last we'd secured.

Technology behind, cursed with its faults,
This step new—yet how decrepit, run-down $_{20}$
It seemed, as even upside down I caught

First views of this ... not-city, half-dead town!
For all that something in me clicked—I knew
This place, and knowing I felt myself groan.

'Virgil,' I cried, 'tell me, and tell me true,
What name this place has; after, let me stand.'
He cleared his throat. 'You know—you see the clues:

Those rackety spires of Oxford, there beyond;
All dreamy with their promises of height,
As Rome on Pontine marshes and swamp ponds; *30*

In truth, all their deep learning obscures light.
Cubicles, portacabins, structures temp,
Pretending education's more than slight.'

With that he hauled me up with easy strength.
'But tell me now,' he said, 'you know this school;
I burn to know before we see its stamp

Just what you saw—your brain beguiled and boiled
Both, in an ecstasy and terror not
Like that which Aeneas felt, or our gods rule;

Something else—that One you mentioned whose knot *40*
No-one or thing unties; eternity's self
Has failed to fathom what His will keeps shut—

And even now to think breaks me in half:
che lungamente m'ha tenuto in fame,
So hungering now as one in a deep fast ...'

He gripped my wrist so firmly, for his aim
Was heaven and at last to see that face
Angels, too, ached to see, and say that Name

Salvation meant, prolific with its grace.
Now Dante turned, delighted hearing words— *50*
His own—great Virgil, exact in his phrase,

Before his own Latin, clearly preferred.
'I saw,' I said, 'what cannot be pronounced
And—' as the image started—within stirred

Once more what overwhelmed, like I'd been lanced
Before, compelling consciousness' retreat—
To look full-on, who could? A mere side-glance

Maybe, the most—unsteady on my feet,
I swayed uncertain whether I could stand,
Could say, would babble or as dumb sheep, bleat— 60

To conjure that image, so far beyond
What I or anyone might grasp, possess.
'The world's a speck, the cosmos a mere pond

And there's a body, pierced and on a cross,
But what I saw but couldn't bear to see:
Such a man face risen from his own death.'

Saying it so, sounded like liberty,
Which indeed so it was, the ultimate;
But such a cost and so what? All for me?

Around me fellow travellers and our fate: 70
To climb till reaching that point we could look
Unwavering upon His immortal state.

But now, who could that passion bear or brook?
That moment when all death and all of hell
Agonised in surprise as He then spoke!

That moment the liar, dragon, just fell
Who'd brought Him down and crushed Him underfoot;
Or so they thought, as He undid their spell

And made of no account the knowing fruit;
Or rather used it as one might a nail$_{80}$
To hold against a wall—and at One's suit—

One whole fragile frame, as in a caul
The baby is—new creation to be born—
Though pierced at first, but that upholds its Fall

Incredibly reversing what pulls down:
How bright the picture now, how full of life
That never ends, that which only He owns.

I stopped my reverie, aware its drift
And wonderment would paralyse me here,
Not moving when God's will is: I persist.$_{90}$

Turning to Virgil, 'We are nearly there,'
He said. We entered a dismal building then,
Low hung with endless plastic corridors,

Sere yellow, dun brown, colours of decline,
Abundant in their wealth of human decay.
We reached a swing door and with it a sign:

'The Head of Education, Kier, B.A.'
I gasped. 'It cannot be—it's forty years
Since Kier ...' and entering, there he lay.

How changed, oh utterly how changed, I swear! *100*
Enfeebled on what seemed a make-shift pallet,
Some ragged rug pulled over—heck, a bier

In all but name, though for him a permanent billet.
He heard the clatter of my feet, raised eyes,
A wan smile crossed his face and hint of scarlet—

Embarrassed to be seen so lacking promise
Compared with that giant whom once he was.
'Welcome, though now you find me in extremis,

For which apologies—to stand, alas,
I cannot, so weakened, but who are these, *110*
Your friends? Welcome to them.' And then he paused.

I saw his eyes in particular seized
On Ness as if that presence meant much more.
But Dante understood all subtleties, wheezes

By which obliques find what they're looking for.
As Virgil laid Ness' body on the ground,
Dante replied, 'We go where you once soared—

Remember? Education's high-pitched mound—
To change the world and make equality
No dream but something even children find? — *120*

As if!—utopias despise history—
Look at yourself now—what virus is it
Lays you this low so that you cannot see

Even a vista of the future's writ?
What does your blanket hide that covers so
A spectacle your being won't permit?'

At these bold words—blow scarlet, hello snow!—
A death-like sweat drenched every facial pore,
And his voice, glottal-stopped, seemed stuck in slow

As struggling he essayed to explain more. *130*
Before he could, Dante just whisked away
The rug that covered, dropped it on the floor:

Two hind flanks and hooves stretched out—listless lay—
Bereft of yore's strength and much more beside:
For here there was no human DNA!

No! Other substance—Ness too had sought to hide,
Explaining Kier's amazement seeing him,
(Carcass attached, like someone who had died).

How could that be—for Ness, a child in prime,
The outcome of what *Education* meant?
Not their destiny to fall, but to climb? *140*

Then Kier gave out a howl which pierced and rent
Air with its soul-sobbing and broken sound.
I felt such pity—who'd not?—for him then;

So my knees bent, and with my arms around
His shoulder sought his comfort. He'd been once
Teacher indeed, but now on other ground,

As all delusions that humans advance
Gave way to evidence his own eyes saw
At last—without beliefs obscuring sense.

But more I comforted, so wept he more. *150*
Some inconsolable grief attacked his being,
A parasite worm burrowing to his core.

Till Dante, beside—knowing Kier was fleeing
Within his deepest depths—now took command:
'The love-child of your life, see here, is dying,

Will die unless you take your proper stand.
Herakles' arrow's struck you, and it is one
Fashioned from futures you yourself had planned.

Irony! Battles fought back then you won;
However, the great war was always lost— *160*
Refusing, as you did, the call of One;

Oh yes, those intellects high, and eyes of lust,
Lust of the flesh, and high the pride of life,
But Ness reveals what you thought good is bust.

So end resistance, end the futile strife—
StairWell is means and method of escape;
Within you a parasite needs its knife—

Stop bending the knee to learning's vast waste,
Cut out that snake to which your mind devotes
Itself; there is a heaven and it is graced *170*

By no serpent whose tongue flickers *Woke*.'
As my arm wrapped Kier's shoulder, Dante now
Touched mine in seemingly a simple stroke,

But as he did, I felt my being glow—
New energy surged through me into Kier—
I, then, the channel which mercy might allow?

His sobbing stopped—collected, he was 'here'.
But hesitant at first, as seeking self-control,
Till finally his words rang out, choke-clear.

'Dear James, I knew you well back at the school—*180*
You such a novice then, an ingenue,
I used for my career, and you my fool.

But—' Here he paused, and raised his eyes to view
Me, fully attentive, as not before,
'No-one else learnt as fast, I'm sure, as you:

Truly, amazed, your progress, who could score?
Each pedagogic metric you surpassed,
And teaching—how few could ever teach more!'

I bowed my head, grateful for praise at last,
Though conscious of the blots that stained my way,*190*
How at the end I'd have nothing to boast—

A pilgrim merely who'd zig-zagged and strayed,
Yet led through mercy to the Throne above;
It seemed unreal—so high for mortal clay.

But Kier resumed: 'To be the best I strove
As well, professional and personal,
And kidded myself all was done for love;

Suffering here, however, drenched in gall
That wanting to exceed the ordinary
Produced, I see my love's no love at all—₂₀₀

I see poor Ness so near to death, and me
So similar—bedazzled by learning's light
So-called—devoted, and like him, to die.'

And there his voice failed, cracked, beneath the weight
Of what to understand his senses came.
'The God you preach—and know—I simply hate

And always have; my life rejects his Name;
Thus now, entrapped on this StairWell, no chance
To move on, progress, I see all is vain.

But yet your touch, and Dante's, made me wince—₂₁₀
I felt the energy surge through, you call grace
I can never have—where's the evidence?

It tells me, calls me to another place;
Those words from long ago—those I believe:
No greater love than this may a man face:

To lay down his life so his friend might live.'
With this he spoke no more. With one impulse
Stood, stretched his hands forward, as if he grieved,

Then clasped the body with its near-dead pulse
And to Ness' thin blue-lips blew in his breath—*220*
With all his being, love, with nothing false.

It seemed obscene, one such embracing death;
To stop him, but myself was stopped instead,
For Dante's arm curled round me like a wreath:

I could but watch, helpless, where Keir's breath led.
At first nothing, except the exhalation's
Repetitive blow, and unrequited feed,

For Ness shared no requisite inspiration;
Rather, as he continued Kier grew pale
Till colours matched and they seemed one creation!*230*

Just at that point, a noise—the StairWell rolled—
As thunder overwhelmed the rational mind—
A typhoon blasting an unbreakable sail

Causing the Earth to shift, now unconfined.
'Look up,' said Dante—there we saw the stars,
So beautiful, and hanging there a sign

From God. Distracted so, who thought of fear?
Or saw how Kier and Ness became one soul?
Oh! Rush of light to suddenly appear—

Its waves like X-rays rippled through us all—*240*
A moment—life's whole riddle, mere child's play!
I gasped in ecstasy, cloaked in its stole,

So that all torments by which I'd been flayed
Throughout existence and its entirety
Displaced themselves like scars that fade away;

That stole forever there, protecting me.
But that was just the start—above the skies
Began to light anew with energies

Irrational, lengthless as number pi,
Solution unexpected in extreme: $_{250}$
The two dissolved into a flow of chi—

And popping into the backdrop's black mean
Fresh stars appeared, as bright as blue and white,
Forming a pattern of a deepening scene:

The Archer at the Milky Way's Great Rift
Grew larger—arrow pointing harder still
At Antares' massive and death-red drift

In Scorpio. Imagine it—the thrill!
For one last time I saw Kier's face within,
And then it changed as Ness—both there to heal— $_{260}$

Held sway, their faces mutually alternating
Amongst the highest stars above; and there
To be ... until more grace ended their waiting.

To see the majesty—and love, who bears?
But now the typhoon's strength eased off, the sail
Of the world returned to its normal steer,

The skies closed, and sweet light began to fail;
And we were on the StairWell still in dark.
Speechless, I choked, felt cheated and derailed.

My turn: 'Why? Why?' I cried, lost in the murk$_{270}$
Of feelings height and depth had addled hard;
Even heavenward, it seemed, some sharp sting lurked.

'My James,' said Virgil, kindly with his words,
'Limbo is worse—and though I feel your pain,
How glad I am to be with you, and spurred

To this hero's quest that we will attain
By that God's grace whom you believe, whom once
I did not, yet ahead the road is plain.'

Then Dante spoke, and more I felt the dunce:
'The Power that moves all things has no short arm,$_{280}$
Is not constricted by fate or by chance;

Did you not see the scorpion's alarm,
That even huge Antares shuddered when
Our Archer aimed his arrow at his harm?

Hidden within the scorpion's death for men
An eagle broods and nests upon an egg
Which John's Apocalypse prophesies open:

And all of Satan's stolen bag of swag
Will be returned to those God raises up;
Meanwhile, we watch His miracles, agog$_{290}$

With wonder.' I raised my eyes: how far the top?
Together then we sought the higher slope.

CANTO 6: LOST FRIEND

The Argument:

Leaving education (because one rather seeks wisdom) proves more difficult than expected. At first, they all seem lost. Virgil finds a blocked tunnel that seems to lead nowhere, but on hearing a tapping sound, a long-lost friend helps them excavate a way forward, and lowers a home-made rung to enable them to climb the fifth stair. At first all seems friendly, but Dante upsets the friend, Kastor, and reveals a secret hidden in the stone itself which Kastor does not want to acknowledge. As Joshua did at Jericho, so the pilgrims break down the stone wall and Kastor gets to meet his long-lost twin soul. Dante has a special affinity with Gemini and body and soul are re-united.

But easier said than done, for to escape
This level's rubric is no easy feat—
Denying as such what our culture shapes,

Which in one metaphor we call learning's seat;
Pervading each assumption is: learning's good,
Regardless there's no wisdom in the West.

We strayed here, then there; even Virgil's mood
Turned sour, and did great Dante know the way?
The while within I hungered for real food,

Not slogans, memes, and self-serving clichés *10*
By which establishments lock in their fools,
Dole out awards, confetti as their pay.

But each road we took—turned—another wall
Reared up its bleak and dead-end face. No hope.
As if to mock—we didn't know it all;

Perhaps if we'd learnt more we might elope,
Escape, together, be rid of this place:
Seat truly—how immobile learning's scope!

At last, we came to where we slowed our pace:
The ceiling lowered, constrained, we hunched down; *20*
Narrower too, it seemed a builder's base—

Plastered in random patches of their own
Were blobs of dried cement, and a plumb rule,
Plus mason's square but made of human bone,

Assorted trowels, chisels, other tools.
But tools or no, ahead seemed wholly blocked,
Diminishing to a point a flea would fail

To pass through. Surely not—encased, enlocked,
With no way back, was this to be our end?
The thought of it unsaid—but still it shocked; 30

So Virgil, raging, struck the ceiling's bend
Just at its furthest point of reach from us,
And as he did—almost overextend—

A tapping sound, exact and without fuss,
Returned an echo to Virgil's hot rage.
We stood dumbstruck—where was, and who was this?

The other side—perhaps a theatre's stage,
With curtains blocking a life hid from view,
Till last, like Oz, we get to see the mage?

I sensed somehow—whatever—Dante knew, 40
Held back some deeper knowledge of this height
We now were at—but how would we break through?

Dante might see with more than mortal sight;
But Virgil—near full in his human form
On our ascent—so struck the board with weight,

Again, again—his message in a storm:
Help us, please, each blow iterated hard
In frantic search for a haven of calm.

It seemed all desperate, hopeless. Then, a word,
Distant at first, but growing louder till 50
A name repeated, *Kastor*, we three heard;

And as we did, we strained for more, stock-still.
Yes, *Kastor coming soon* its voice intoned;
And louder grew that voice, persistent will.

Something like a drill sounded on thick stone—
Harsh, shrill—succeeded by deft hammer blows,
Each stronger still, blasting heavy stone down.

Finally, cracking open the fascia's show,
Allowing duller light through where we stood
Amazed, fine powder drifting down also. *60*

'Come on, lads,' Kastor's voice, 'don't stand like wood;
I've cracked the rock—dismantle piece by piece
Your end. I'll lower a ladder I've made.'

Instantly mobilised by this new lease
Of hope, we reached our hands to clasp the stone
Fragments to lever each lump's awkward release.

How feverishly we worked, and not alone,
For we heard Kastor digging at his end,
So, after some short time, a hole was done;

Through it we saw our rescuer's face—our friend— *70*
Who now dropped down his home-made ladder's rungs
That we might climb above learning's trapped strand.

How friendly Kastor, and eager to bring
Us to a new and safe surface, his home;
Emerging—though behind, sealed with a bung,

He closed the cell from which we had just flown,
Which I for one did not understand why;
Indeed, why not want the route to be known

That others too ascend through to the sky?
But breathless, grateful, I set thoughts aside—$_{80}$
Distracted, laughing, Kastor, a good guy.

Here humour reigned and good will circled wide.
Before I—or we—could thank our host for aid
So timely given, skilfully applied,

Kastor began a story that he'd made,
Insisting every word, of course, was true:
We learnt the pointing of each brick he'd laid.

Invited to admire his structured view,
We could not help but see, for sure, how well
Constructed—seamless, solid, seeming new—$_{90}$

This landscape was, though for me, truth to tell,
Despite its technical accomplishments,
I'd rather live somewhere more natural.

Still, everywhere I looked he'd clearly spent
Untold effort and time getting it right,
At least for him—I wondered where it went?

'Kastor—impressive, ahead what a sight!
But tell me—' before, though, my question's out,
I'm misdirected by a verbal sleight—

Some whimsy, quibble that his mind's about. *100*
He blurts with glee, 'Remember, Jim, that bar?'
Then laughing, 'That girl whom you tried to date?

You had style—only twelve steps—but so far
With everyone watching, you cool as ice,
Her "No", and you, just as coolly, retire.'

Perhaps—so fascinating, the old topic,
And him parading what he knew—was there—
It seems no end to talking—of my vice!

But Dante now, 'Kastor—we seek the stair
Where we can climb and reach the chapel of *110*
St Luke's—the last point of purgatory here?'

'There is no other level, no above,'
Said Kastor curtly—Dante's tone—direct,
Urgent—implied rebuke, and him not chuffed.

Now Dante stared, unwavering to correct
The falsehood that he'd heard. I noticed then
Something before too subtle to detect:

His eyelids never winked, were always open
As if to never block one ray of light
From entering, increasing his spirit's span. *120*

Poor Kastor tried returning sight for sight,
As some playground bully seeks to outface
That newcomer who dominates in height,

Whose power matches too-evident grace.
But his gaze breaks, and mumbling adds, 'Maybe,
There was a spot once, here, another place,

It's sealed up, surely, for health and safety.'
Then finally, 'It's best we're on our own.'
With that he draws back, moves away from me—

Regretting that he'd let us in his home, *130*
Afraid he'd let slip some secret in his soul,
Or he'd be found deficient in his sums?

Whatever calculation held control,
I saw him squirm, reverse away from us,
Leaving sound-silence drape us in its pall,

But silence not diminishing Dante's prowess—
'Listen,' he said, hand raised, finger a quill
About to write a word—what word?—*quietus?*

Nothing at all, but then I felt a chill,
My eyes—as ears—directed to stonework, *140*
Some minor spot not seeming good or ill

Unblemished, almost sub-audible, I heard
Groaning within, some dryad not in trees
But stuck in stone instead, and stuck here hard—

A sobbing, weeping, finding no release
As if in stone there was no place for tears—
As if ... in stone I'd find some missing piece!

'No! Not there!' Kastor, in anguish and fear
Suddenly exclaimed, shrivelling up, paralysed,
Unable, though, to get away from here _150_

Where he least sought to be. I realised,
Turning to him—though by now so removed
He seemed—something in him, profound, died,

Or so he thought had—which was but engraved,
Lost in this rock, that our presence now stirred
From depths—for Dante's life it sensed and craved.

'What have you done?' said Master stern—and whirled
Round on the hapless Kastor, crouching as
Some beaten dog might, knowing how he'd erred,

Fearing a further whipping. 'What it is,' _160_
He whimpered, 'simply, I don't remember;
It's not my fault—you know,' he begged, 'time flies;

I—we—forget, between there's so much slumber;
Who can recall what long is past and gone?'
But Dante was long bored by this dissembler;

Had turned again, faced where the sound in stone
Came from; there felt a while each saddening note,
His hand against the wall and focused on

The barriers to love built up by hate.
'Quickly, your instruments,' he barked command. _170_
I had no idea by this what he meant,

But Kastor knew, as if it were all planned
From all eternity. He scuttled off;
Within minutes presented, with full hands,

Gingerly, four misshapen trumpets, scuffed
And dusty, used once, perhaps, never more,
Barely, for music, were they good enough.

But Dante now aligned us on the floor;
Reluctant, Kastor took his place. We faced
The wall and Dante said, 'Think this a door; *180*

Beyond's a human soul that's been laid waste;
Now stamp together, blow some seven times,
And when I say shout, *shout*; here I am priest.'

So we began—how strange the trumpets' chimes
Which almost weren't, yet with each blast
Weird euphony increased and volume climbed,

Especially each stamp harder than the last,
Till finally we shouted, 'Elohim!'
In one tremendous surge—as plaster casts

Crack, so the wall fell down—and we saw him, *190*
Frozen in crystalline, too cold to shiver,
Too weak to speak, but if a painter limned

His outline, Kastor's Double he'd deliver
Exactly. We all gasped; as peeling from
The wall this Double keeled—a shadow—over

Onto the floor, collapsing from its womb,
But touching ground instantly had effect:
Like Antaeus who gained strength from his home—

The Earth—so here, though a different connect
(For this floor underlay the heavenly route);$_{200}$
Now effortless, the Double stood erect,

All cold gone and god-like as summer fruit,
As ripe. Now Virgil, overwhelmed it seemed—
Astounded—'Dioscuri', blurted out,

Adding substance to the shadow he'd named.
Now Pollux smiled, as long ago he had
When, masterfully, Cyllarus he'd tamed.

'Yes,'—proudly—'I'm Pollux,' he said aloud,
'And this no brother but closer—my twin—
Who sadly tricked me, lost me in this shroud$_{210}$

Of stone—shed his soul, as a snake its skin,
Foregoing then immortal life for this:
A perfect match-box he's fashioned within.'

With that he gestured, as one might dismiss
As irrelevant the suffering before;
Now was the opportunity not to miss!

'Brother,' he said, 'I'm what your body's for,
I'm your immortal part we call the soul;
How long lost—locked in self-created doors—

You've been. But see—once more we can be whole.'[220]
With this his arms upraised as to embrace
Kastor, who shrank in terror from his call—

Truly, as if Medusa he'd more face
Than bone of his bone, and blood of his blood—
A join once severed, thought to leave no trace,

Proved otherwise; what makes a fracture good?
What causes such clefting of the soul from flesh?
Or fear divide two cells from the same brood?

But Kastor's delay for me induced a rush—
His fear contaminated, shed its sweat[230]
Like oil (in some bike shop) whose oozings crush

Into the fabric of the wooden seats—
If I—or we—were to make paradise
Resentment in my heart I'd have to break

And quickly. 'Kastor, know, your brother's right:
Too long the box has held you in its thrall—
The Rules, the Regs, follow instructions quite

To be beyond reproach; what good at all
Is that? Imagine, as I know you can,
Another world, and one without a Fall;[240]

Where you and I can talk as man to man;
Where secret fears hold no pernicious sway:
At last to be before the Throne—and stand!

Forgive me, then, for what I failed to say
Or do those years I had your confidence;
Together let's be up and on our way.'

But words provide no solid evidence
That things are other than what we believe:
So Kastor crouched trembling, would not advance,

Or make the least step to gain some relief. *250*
In desperation, then, to shift his pose
I rummaged where the tool-kit had been left

And found a mirror—what was there to lose?
Before him—before his face—I said, 'Look—
Your face—and see, Pollux, how his one goes?

Identical!' His eyes swivelled, as spooked
By what he saw, as if for the first time;
Perhaps, at last—his mind now engaged—hooked

By truth which he could finally call, 'Mine'.
He stirred—out from terror's overwhelm—*260*
Then Dante added his own words, divine:

'Kastor, the stars are where we look, our helm
To guide us out and up, though here we're blocked
For now, yet know I share with you your realm

Of Gemini—am born beneath its clock's
Celestial motion and power of the air;
Like Libra, Aquarius, all have double shock's

Duality—most certainly: the Pair;
Also, Man with his Pail too, and two Scales,
In us division is the atmosphere $_{270}$

We breathe ascending; no time now to fail;
Take Pollux's hand and see yourself what sign
Awaits you—sky itself will be your Grail.'

So Pollux, as with Dante's words, aligned
Himself—outstretched hand tempting Kastor take,
Which—cumulative properties combined—

He did—and surged upwards, no longer weak;
Instead, I saw the two meld into one.
'Brother!' both said, but who was first to speak

I couldn't say; one loud laugh—it was done; $_{280}$
Talking to himself, one said, 'This is fun!'

CANTO 7: FIGHTER

The Argument:

Kastor has fused with his own twin, immortal soul, Pollux. Now the pilgrims must resume their journey upwards. The Dioscuri choose the wrong direction, but fate intervenes and they turn right. A barking dog leads them in a pathless, dark maze which finally reveals itself as arriving on the sixth stair where they find Dan Fast, the poet's old mentor and trainer, in fatal combat with a Minotaur. There at the point of exhaustion and defeat, Pollux within the Dioscuri manifests himself and moves to save Dan Fast. In one decisive martial action Pollux prevails. Dan is amazed by his skill but Dante insists on not lingering. The stars above configure and show that the Dioscuri and Dan must go a separate way to the pilgrims. With sorrow and regret they part.

That Dioscuri simply punched a hole

Where latterly the half of him had been
Entrapped—threadbare as a wallpaper roll

The stone wall split, and we witnessed the scene
Ahead: an azure dragon painted, pointing,
It's head one lane right, tail to leftward leaned.

Two ways to go, but which one led to mounting,
Reaching the chapel? Dark alleyways both;
Should we divide, as climbers on a mountain

Split fellowship though parting so is loath, *10*
With dread of their uncertainty increased,
Numbers declined to face alternative truths?

Now Dante stepped forward, and not best pleased,
Inspected where the opening gaped wide—
Who else might know, had his deep expertise?

Yet heaven help! Wavered to go inside—
So, Dioscuri then piped up, more sure:
'We turn to left—what matter, seize the tide,

All roads to Rome lead is the iron law.'
At which mention of Rome, recalling wonders *20*
Lost, Virgil stirred, knew such roads long before,

And signalled 'Yes', forgetting Rome's past blunders:
Its pagan, godless tracks ending nowhere
But where barbaric tribes ripped it asunder;

And where also dark catacombs interred
Those worshipping another God had rest—
Not like above—but as their hope, all buried,

Till comes that other Day they wait; at least
They must have told the Emperor so their lore,
As thumbs-down consigned most of them to death;30

But waiting, still they wait, wait for the door
That opens out from gloom and Rome's despair
Towards another Sovereign's golden shore.

Then I could almost feel them in the air,
As if from Rome's ruins they still took breath,
For what could kill the true hope that was theirs?

As if in answer, then, though lost beneath
Time's broken masonry, I heard them sigh
Collectively, which rattled the whole Earth—

Its tremor thoroughly swept through purgatory;40
Brickwork ahead fell out in fragments, shards,
And—far-fetched—formed an arrow in their lie.

We stood dumb-struck, amazed: the left was barred;
The pointer said to right is the right way;
Only blackguards played odds against clear stars.

The Dioscuri shrugged, no joy to stay
Or argue that our choices didn't matter
For Fate deemed otherwise. Without delay

We entered darkness (and not without a shudder),
Turning to right as seemed the way, and each [50]
Reached out to guide—in single file—the other.

For Dante led, upfront, also in speech:
His quiet words, a comfort—like a hum
Of bees whose flowers soon will be in reach.

As smaller steps wound round a sharpening climb—
Like one might feel scaling a lighthouse top—
I traipsed last, relieved to be behind,

In Virgil's hand, mine, but—to go or stop?
We'd gotten Purgatory's mid-point—so much
Success, but then—so high, so far to drop! [60]

I couldn't help but note from Virgil's touch
An energy ran as from Dante's source
Downwards to me, as in me to debouch,

Celestial power dissipating its force—
How weak the flesh to contain heaven's fire,
Unless the One Himself touches, of course.

Such thoughts, as Virgil dragged me higher,
Wrestled within my soul, weakening resolve,
Why strain this way, scenarios more dire

Each one than the last—could not God absolve [70]
Directly, quit me of this need to grasp
His heights? Would it mean His justice shelved

To give me—through His mercy—a free pass?
As mounting, so my mind kept sliding back,
Till suddenly a noise, a vicious rasp—

Or was it more an urgent, repeated yap
As of some dog who, standing guard, would like
But would not through fear conduct an attack:

Ahead one too many pilgrims to strike
Perhaps. As now we reached a pooling space,$_{80}$
A level spread out like a rink of ice,

Behind it darkness concealing a maze,
And at its edge a backward-stepping dog
Which snarled incessantly—its only phrase—

Hostile, alarmed, though in its tone, a beg
We follow into the blackness stretched behind.
There seemed no other way, no time to flag,

So Dante led us into this deep blind,
And all the while as darkness palpably
Reached out and touched us in its whole surround,$_{90}$

Only the dog's perpetual bark meant we
Had some sense other than the nothingness
By which we seemed encompassed, unwillingly.

Again, we turned, and turned through more abyss;
The sound that had seemed so cruel and sharp
Being the only reality left us to bless,

Began almost to reassure as on it harped.
I cannot count how many steps we trod
And wished a thread might take us back to start

If in this blackness no path led to God. *100*
But just as soul within, about to faint—
Give up—there crackled bellicose ahead

Another sound which added its layered paint
To all the textured gloom in which we moved
So feebly, lacking in drive or real want.

At first, so difficult as light allowed
To see what beings shuffled restlessly
Across a dirt patch fighting, both unbowed.

But now just as sight became clear to me,
The barking stopped and that dog—more wolf-hound—*110*
Spun round, not backwards, not like he would flee;

I saw its glory, strategy come round:
Loyalty to its master, near wits' end,
Strength too, and there in the centre, near down—

Where that colossal Minotaur crushed Dan—
Now out of tricks to wrestle free—the dog
Had brought us to see and help his one man;

And now we had: he bounded—like a stag—
And before the Minotaur's coup de grace
Savaged and bit hard into his hind leg. *120*

Instantly, the beast's roar consumed the place;
We—Dante excepted—needs block our ears;
As we did, saw Dan dropped flat on his face.

Enraged the creature turned attention where
The brave hound hung perilous on its flank.
Malevolent—horns like two scimitars,

He shifted balance and with one sharp stroke
One loyal dog yelped and fell into three
Pieces. I heard Dan moan—his spirit broken,

But then he staggered up, and found his feet, *130*
This one last time he'd try the odds and die
With honour. 'Come on,' he yelled, viciously.

That beast now relished this—he had his guy
Full at his mercy—one longer, last charge—
The Minotaur moved back so he could fly

Straight at Dan. How heaven, though, disobliges
The certain. Suddenly, the Dioscuri
Slid forward, fearsome with purposed urge—

Some psychic wave, but revealed to the eye,
Made Minotaur turn; and there to behold *140*
Another human and adversary.

Almost I thought that bestial face's fold
Smiled with some low cunning I'd never plumb;
Poor Dan, near blind from dust, yet while strength held

Watched—impressed, by one not yet overcome.
Stamping his feet, the beast now reared its form,
Ran straight at Dioscuri, hooves hard to thrum—

And Virgil gasped—did even Dante squirm?—
My breath congested its own livingness
As if no longer air, but congealed phlegm. *150*

Near twice the size held that beast's large prowess;
How small the Dioscuri, patient in his walk,
Unerring in his confidence, I guess.

A millisecond before the shattering torque
Of Minotaur destroyed our friend, the Twin,
Just then—not Kastor within but Pollux

Appeared in one martial move of lightning:
Impossible, his fist struck Minotaur
Packed on the nose, or rather its bull-like rim,

And down dead instantly, the monster floored! *160*
Dan Fast, the master, barely believed it;
Collapsing to his knees—what his eyes saw!—

'Show me,' he cried, 'Are you real, this a trick?
I must know.' Forgotten his dog—pure awe
Now overwhelmed his senses, addled wits.

'So long,' said Virgil, 'in Limbo's arid jaw—
What matter Homer and others discuss
Their poetry, even poetry of war,

When I now feel in flesh again the lust
For victory over darkness and its spawn.' *170*
His face no longer white but red as rust,

The blood in him rushing, almost re-born,
To be a living man rising to God.
I could not help but hold him in my arms—

Weeping, we wept together for this good.
Just when defeat had seemed inevitable,
The One who holds the Scales had turned the flood:

In dust the Minotaur all dead, disabled!
But who was he, and where had he come from?
'A monster from the depths'—that label—cancelled? *180*

What depths? How deep, how monstrous and strong?
As thoughts like these obsessed me—Virgil too—
Dante advanced to where Dan Fast lay strung

Out on the floor, done-in by fight, kung-fu,
And overwhelm of his lost dog, his friend.
His conflict over, what was he to do?

Somewhere in the middle points to no end;
Yet time goes on—his place set out—a gym,
Or dojo for training in which hard men

Practised their mastery; there we'd seen him— *190*
My old master, the great Dan Fast himself,
Black belt and more, as we'd gained access in.

But whatever he had been, now time's stealth
Subtracted all his great vitality
And skill-set, foundation of his life's wealth—

Hardly could he stand, both wonky his knees,
So much the fighting now and years, wore down,
And what heart wanted, body couldn't please.

But discipline—its sheer rigour he owned.
Now, 'James, so welcome back—you've come to train?$_{200}$
Your friend there, what did you say his name?'

He laughed, exhausted as he was—again
Though, bad habits die hardest in the strong—
To even think to spar with Pollux vain,

Still wanting to know, though, secrets he'd sprung!
A teacher ever learning some new trick—
'I'm fast,' he grinned, 'but who could match your prong?

Can you teach me—that move you did's unique?
My knees are not what they were: solid steel—
Titanium—clunkier and less slick ...'$_{210}$

But Dante interposed—no time for deals
Between the masters of the boxing art;
For him ahead was where the Power was real.

'In ancient times the Masters knew their part;
Were one with forces invisible, hidden,
So deep, impossible to plumb their heart,

They moved though, moved as eternity bid them,
And recognised forbearance as the first
Which led to justice ... then mastery's side room,

An ante-chamber of Heaven where durst$_{220}$
They go to find the very soul of Tao;
To scrap here endlessly is to be cursed.

These stars above configure, tell you 'Go';
A greater prize awaits you if you climb—
The Tao has countless names in which it flows—

See there, beside the Twins, Orion's prime
Position where—no adder in the path—
Immortal Hunter be your paradigm;

Though first, you'll need to wrestle with the truth.'
His words impacted me as much as Dan:$_{230}$
Star-struck, Fast stood and stared at the sky's roof

For proof that Dante's words might prove his plan—
What confirmation could that be, indeed?
He saw the pointer: the Belt's triple line

And gazing at it his soul seemed to feed;
Whilst I, in contrast, contracted in my shell;
What pointed Dan to his real, higher need,

Reminded me not of stars, but a well
Of cowardice with which my past was shamed:
One time, me sixteen in a gaming hall—$_{240}$

A friend in trouble called for help—my name—
Some big bruiser on his back, about to beat
Him black and blue, and I as one new-lamed,

Unable to stand up or stir my feet:
Sheer fear within—I knew the bruiser, Bob,
A full-on lout whom I'd never dare hit;

Unlike Dan who'd give Bob all that he'd got.
Remember James, you turned so not to hear?
No champion then, about to take his shot!

How hopeless, useless, and dumb-struck with fear;₂₅₀
Whilst all the while beside me Dan stood calm;
How different emotions both, I swear,

Except, at last, Dan's voice broke in alarm,
And I too knew he felt what I had felt—
Fear; only mine inaction from deep shame,

But his, a rousing of some long-lost guilt
Which Orion's belt now pointed to, beyond:
He croaked, tremulous, as if to the hilt

Some two-edged sword into his mind were plunged—
'The Master! Dividing my spirit, soul—₂₆₀
Each star against me glowing, me arraigned,

And Him so fast, His movements, perfect, whole:
Who stands?' With that his knees dropped down, like lead
Weighted into water from a fisher's reel,

Awestruck, seeming paralysed in his head;
Still gazing up—at what, we might not see.
Then Dante's hand, soft as a silken thread,

Stretched out and touched his hair so tenderly,
Chivvying, massaging life back again;
As he did so—to watch—my fear left me.$_{270}$

Dioscuri stepped up to take the reins:
'St Luke's ahead is not where we Twins rest;
There Dante must lead both Virgil and James.

But we, like Dan, are not to be so blessed;
The Minotaur I killed with one mere blow
Is Dan's other half which his life repressed.

Divided, but see us—we are one show!
So, cousin Dan needs help to find his soul—
Only to the stars is the way to go.

We wait with him, as heaven's axle rolls$_{280}$
And One you worship brings His mercy home—
Till stars configure, Dan must pay his toll.'

Virgil and I both looked askance, looked down:
How could we leave our comrades on this road?
But Dante clarified the matter some:

'No more delay—let them have their abode;
We tread a path, another way to Him,
The Way Himself offered hanging on wood.

I know this Way and know where we must climb.'
With tears, we bid farewell, so hard to leave *290*
Those we knew, loved—what were their chances, slim?

Dante, however, moved, no time to grieve;
Perhaps we'd meet again beyond this grave.

CANTO 8: COVID-PRIEST

The Argument:

Regretfully they part from Dan and the Dioscuri. With renewed energy, they press on to the seventh stair where they find themselves in an enormous church nave. Whilst they ponder on its magnificence, a voice (Penny, the Priest's) harshly warns them of the dangers of Covid and of not wearing a mask. Virgil and the poet are intimidated by the priest's presence. But Dante is not. Seeing through the priest's hypocrisy and moral virtue-signalling, he holds an ankh aloft and calls on St Paul's estimation of what happens to those who may be saved, but as through fire. Just in time, Virgil and the poet hit the floor, but Penny does not and experiences the full-blast; however, at the last minute, Penny repents and through Dante re-learns and sings the alphabet of grace. From the church, the next stair moves to the political arena where they discover a blond Titan who is holding up the sky, and seemingly friendly!

How hard it was to step away from them—
Resolved to find that path that led to God;
Determined to pursue no less than Him,

If His will be that we should catch such good
Beyond ever all mortal men deserved
(Especially Virgil and me), who stood

With Dante facing a tunnel which swerved
Abruptly upwards, down which organ sounds
As from a church spilled; but we held our nerve,

Pressed on, as each step our steps unwound; 10
We entered into a marvellous space:
One nave, huge, high-ceilinged, a new-found land

Whose emptiness astonished—a still place,
Designed for worship but more like some crypt
In which humans might be, yet see no face.

Suddenly, as from nowhere, muffled lips
Screeched out a warning almost clear, but tart:
I heard, 'Pandemic on—feet—apart—six—

Or leave!' We shuffled unsure; Dante alert
But Virgil and I experiencing guilt—20
Too close, were we? So, we were causing hurt?

Whose voice was this with its imperious lilt
And caustic accusation? And there she was,
As if up from an altar where she dwelt—

Then magicked into our presence, alas!
'I am the priest in charge—Penny Crow—
Where have you been, and have you had the vax?'

She wore the sacred vestments loose—her cope,
Cassock and tippet, grand finery of church,
So that poor Virgil shrank, felt drained of hope,*30*

That one so high—near God—with God's own stature
From holy garments, Peter's sanction given
To be the Rock on which authority perched—

How then, without her blessing, get to heaven?
Poor Virgil—used to power, imperial-bent,
But only that type which is earthly driven;

His hopes all now above, how strange Crow's rant,
But sensing some divine rebuke within,
Taken aback by reprimand's raw cant,

How down he seemed. But what was, wasn't sin*40*
Immortal Dante knew, who'd seen God's face.
'I come,' he said, 'to lead these from ruin,

To where the chapel of St Luke is placed,
Not here—where desolation's to be found—
But where at last their solace will be tasted.'

Why! Reverend Crow, open-mouthed, astounded;
Did not this new-comer trespass her domain?
Was that her teeth—who else's—we heard ground?

'Excuse me, you are?' she said, annoyed, plain
Disturbed, so that why bother be polite: 50
Her "Jesus" enjoined not that rule or strain?

Besides, just who was this spirit of ... light?
She flinched as before whom she addressed glowed,
Such that her certainties mind held took flight;

Some dubious fog appearing danger showed;
Be careful—we saw her heart shrivel back
Into its desiccated shell of pride,

Not wanting to commit now to attack
Until identity was clarified—
Suppose this *angel*, bishop—what bad luck! 60

'I was a man once,' Dante said, 'but died;
Before I did, I wrote about the Popes,
Corruption in the church, and thus not shied

Away from scolding killers of Christ's hope:
That all the world might be saved, saved through Him'—
I felt it, Virgil too, a tremor's throb,

As if he had in naming of His name—
For one instant revealed—nothing stood;
Nothing could stand, for all existence lame;

The living too—all frozen in their blood 70
And toppled. Myself, I felt panic rise
In that recess where heart finds little good,

Wanting to cry: 'Cover me—blind my eyes—
Oh, everlasting hills be my refuge!
Lest I should see the One the world despised—

And die.' Now kneeling, Virgil like some stooge
To my own actions (we both stupefied)
Raised arms as if he were some thaumaturge

Who rearing mercy (the while petrified)
Perhaps might hope *only* grace limitless$_{80}$
When faith and love in us had never died

Because—as sinners in our own long chaos,
They'd never lived. And then a stillness held,
Abrupt and sudden, quiet as green moss,

Replaced the quake, unfinished and untold;
A dream we had maybe, vision to come—
When finished fully God's plan would unfold.

For now, though, we sat back, both dazed and dumb.
Above us, sensing Dante stood—advanced—
Towards the priest whose own fear—rendered numb—$_{90}$

Unfounded by this calm—at first, she winced
As some reflex to higher truth dismissed,
As one might to a voice heard at a séance;

Then Dante's head near close enough to kiss
Her lips, which to her suddenly loomed;
Outraged, and in recoil, she spluttered, hissed;

(The nave not big enough for all its room!)
'An epidemic's here—put on your mask—
How dare you stand so close, and so presume—'

Before her sentence closed, finished its task $_{100}$
However, Dante's right hand upstretched high
And pointing ceilingward he held an ankh—

From whence it came I knew not—but to the sky
Beyond the roof and steeple its ley lines
Sped on their way, awaiting their reply

Quite instantaneous: ready with His signs—
Dissolving what had seemed solid above,
We saw transparent stars in order shine,

Zodiac rotating on its wheel of love;
Already Virgil, I, were on our knees, $_{110}$
Now Dante fell to his, and there we shelved

Our souls in reverence. But no, not she—
Still standing, looking round witless and lost,
Unable to comprehend what all could see—

The constellation—Aries' shining ghost,
Which momentarily flickered high above,
As if a switch clicked then Aries went ... lost ...

Because these shepherds owed their sheep no love:
Too busy with their own right-on careers,
Too busy fiddling all their woke-riffed moves, $_{120}$

Too busy, busy, for souls living here—
Out from the churches, one by one, they stray,
Chewing philosophies, bleak, false and drear.

'Great God,' cried Dante, 'Your people can't pray:
This place—like Ripon in the north—is closed
To prayer, though they prayed on Black Death days,

And prayed when Europe's Spanish Flu was loosed;
Through each catastrophe and every war
Prayer and sacraments were diagnosed.

But you—glad tidings: Covid's what you hear!$_{130}$
With solemn disappointment tell the flock
For all their sakes your Archbishop's been clear:

So, slam the church door shut; and prayer, put a sock
In it—why, praying, singing songs to God
May spread disease—better God under lock.

And you, you hypocrite, pretending good,
As if you weren't glad not to tend the sheep,
Be done, abolish tedious needs for food:

Communion itself for those whom God keeps—
Beware, for "Jesus" whom you claim to serve$_{140}$
Is not so mocked; and sowing's what you'll reap.

Remember Paul? Don't worry, you'll not starve,
But will—' With that, he paused, and his hand turned,
And pointing the ankh, 'Get what you deserve.'

Something like panic inflamed, deep-like burned
Across her face as the stars drooped to fade,
The roof grew solid, and sensing she'd be harmed,

'Stop praying,' she screeched, 'restrictions forbid!'
But now great Dante stood and held the while
That ankh at her face and said, 'Too late.' *150*

A whisper ... hissing ... as of some gas-spill
Grew in intensity. 'My friends, lie flat.'
Instantly, we obeyed; but she stood tall.

'Hear now,' cried Dante loudly, '... that estate
Saint Paul informs us of—' A sudden blast
Of fire purged through the porch's iron gate

And through the church, consuming in its path
All flesh that it encountered. We, floor-bound,
Only felt the heat above our necks, rasp—

And dare not look, eyes fixed firm to the ground. *160*
But my mind's eye grasped all, sharp as glass is:
Fire burned upwardly, forming one massed mound—

A vaulting pillar just like one before that Moses
Saw—and which led the Israelites across
Vast deadly deserts in their hopeless darkness,

Now settled on her, intending her loss.
As some image viewed, rear-side of my head,
I saw her squirm and squeal as in flames tossed

Her being's atoms started to unthread.
Whatever's unworthy perished in this blaze; *170*
And still beside stood Dante, unperturbed.

Then said a word, or maybe more, a phrase:
'Do you believe?' Screaming in entangled harm,
'I do! I do! I do!' nearly too late;

But soon enough; his ankh freely turned
From minatory to another aspect:
Of light that burned away the fire that burned!

Upon the wall of flame a new prospect
Appeared—a circle, laser cut, as one
Who burgles breaks glass—through his hand irrupts *180*

To lift the inside latch. Now baked and done,
Her desperate hand reached out to touch his sign,
And doing so—grace works!—the pillar's gone.

Collapsing on the stone floor's hard design—
That wreck of former self, yet soul still there,
Preserved as by immortal love's strong bind

That for all perfidy still held all cure,
For those who called on that one name of Christ:
The One whose own Word He cannot forswear.

I saw him: Virgil, his own hair uprist, *190*
As my own body trembled on the floor;
We both aware how near the Master's tryst

113

With her with whom He settled now the score.
I cried out, 'Mercy, Lord,' and hid my head,
Praying the while His Presence would pass over.

As in a sleep, and then one wakes in bed,
Sunshine is streaming through the window pane,
So sensing, I woke to morning's bright thread.

There Penny sat, re-clothed in white, and sane;
Confessing, so it seemed, to Dante beside,₂₀₀
Learning the alphabet of grace again:

ABCs of meaning to be Christ's bride.
In some sweet lull of time—clerestories
Allowing light to stream through reddened sides—

Dante removed himself, to join our story,
And she the while in a high psalm-like song
Continued, satisfied, re-writing history

In light of His great right against her wrong.
We moved to exit but her voice then soared
So that my heart thrilled knowing she belonged₂₁₀

To that heaven where heart is at the core.
How I repented hostile thoughts intended;
I wanted, yes, to stay awhile, hear more.

But go we must, and she—till singing ended
And all transformed to light in Him—must stay.
Ahead, a path from out the church wended

A new direction opposite in way
From where we'd been, now not liturgical,
More powerful, political in sway.

An Arch, all Marble, not far the great White Hall,$_{220}$
Beyond which I saw bureaucratic throngs
In droves obey those whims of one Masterful:

As we approached, I saw him: massively strong,
Herakles, blond yet bulging at the waist,
His hair tousled outrageously, though not long;

Two arms outstretched to balance step in place.
Like Atlas heaving up the sky—on him
So much depended, on him so much weighed.

He spotted us as we ventured right in.
'Hey, chaps—over here—help me hold this thing!'$_{230}$

CANTO 9: HERAKLES

T he Argument:

From the high tension in the church, the eighth stair reveals a god-like, political hero—Herakles—holding up the sky with both hands. Friendly, though, he casually asks for a helping hand, and this the poet moves to provide; but Dante restrains him, and reminds him of Atlas' fate long ago. However, Herakles pleads again, and almost inadvertently the poet reaches out to help, despite Dante's warning. As soon as his hand touches the sky, he is trapped with unbearable pressure. Dante, displeased by the poet's ignoring of his advice, is not inclined to rescue. Only by thinking on his—buckling—feet, does the poet come up with a ruse that saves him. They leave Herakles stuck in his old task. One unexpected benefit of the Covid-virus and mask-wearing is that the crowds are dissipated and there is a clear way through to reach the steep and daunting ninth stair.

How curious, casual our fresh intro was
Into this brave new world Herakles held;
So different from what we had had to pass

Before—those portals: hard core, jinxed and spelled
With magic—sourced supernal—though to those
Trapped on its levels, perhaps darker delved;

But as I mused, that voice once more arose:
'Hey chaps, I mean it, please give us a hand—
The weight of this sends shudders down my toes!'

I smirked—his stuttering address and bland $_{10}$
Request for help, for all his strength, endeared;
And surely, alone, how endure and stand?

I went forward to support, nothing feared,
But before my hand reached up, Dante's reached
Preventing mine, and his stern words soon cleared

My mind of madness' automatic twitch:
'Beware, remember Atlas and his ruse—
How Herakles, helping, found himself glitched;

And switching, Atlas—freed at last—refused;
Only the cunning of divinest wit $_{20}$
Saved Herakles, left Atlas holding, confused;

Without Dante, I'd have fallen for it.
My hand just hesitated in mid-air—
To touch his sky; an unwilling conscript

For an eternity of being there.
'Oh, come on guys,' he said, 'it's not that bad.
A little help from friends is only fair.

I'm following Winston—recall what he did?
It's all about freedom, resisting tyrants;
I've helped the English to become untied$_{30}$

From Europe's pygmies camouflaged as giants,
With all their avaricious grasping for more.
Defying gravity's an art not science:

How much longer between ceiling and floor
Can I—must I—sustain this yawning gap?'
And then his face turned sad, all bleached yet raw.

'I'm at my wits' end, you've got to help, chaps!'
It touched the heart to hear him speak this way.
I asked myself—what possible mishap

Could there be... and as I thought, my hand strayed$_{40}$
Beyond mid-air, and touched the very roof
He held—and so my Dante disobeyed!

Instantly pressure—pounced—swift as a wolf—
My whole being shot through and overwhelmed,
So that without a thought, like some dumb oaf

My second hand raised, touched, and sought to stem
That strain compounding severest-there 'stuck'.
I cried in pain as my eyes beseeched him.

All Herakles could say, though, was, 'What luck!'
As consummate with ease his hands took off $_{50}$
Themselves; he added, 'I thought I was fucked.'

The charm of old Nick or some Etonian toff
Who to the manor born is born not to—
Not try too hard that is, just so their stuff's

Enough. Reflecting—all that I could do—
Diverting attention from crushing pain's
Momentous weight which every second screwed

More on my buckling, overburdened frame.
I didn't want to look but clearly saw
All letters spelling disappointment's name $_{60}$

In Dante's eyes: this drove into my core—
I stumbled, one knee now nobbling the ground,
Bent awkward, usurping what the foot's for.

Then Virgil's voice raised its lamenting sound:
'We must help the poet, or else he'll fall—
Our friend—so close to heaven, now this wound!'

From Dante I heard nothing, nothing at all.
'Must go,' said Herakles, 'nice meeting you.'
Before he did, though, I sneezed, as one ill $_{70}$

Unwillingly, a sudden bout of flu
Or virus more malevolent, invasive;
And Herakles froze, uncertain what to do—

As if some obligation he'd sworn to live
By held him back, or some primeval pact
He'd have to honour, needed to survive ...

Awkwardly, casual and matter of fact,
He leaned backwards with cheery, leery wink,
'You have a mask, my friend, don't say you lack?

I made it policy, Downing-Street-think,[80]
The country bought the message whole, wholesale;
Though didn't mean of course you couldn't drink.

But wearing masks keeps Covid safely filed
Away, reduces deaths, well, experts say,
So, take the vaccine, why live in denial?

And you, why cough and let your mucus spray?
Go on—put on your mask and do your bit.'
'I would,' I groaned, 'but I can't find the way.

My pocket's deep and my mask is in it.
Can you reach in, remove, place it on me?[90]
I'd be so grateful—great king of politics!'

That last phrase, wow, he liked a lot seemingly;
But vast distaste accompanied the thought
Of his hand delving into pickpocketry.

I saw his mind conflicted by not and ought,
So, seizing the high ground before he spoke,
I said, 'My pocket's full-infection fraught;

Unfair to ask your hand to enter—poke
Around therein—why not a simple scheme:
Just hold this roof a mo while my hand looks—*100*

Will take a second; we'll be as we've been;
Sorted.' I scarce believed he'd take the bait,
But sometimes simpletons fool subtle men.

'OK,' he said, 'But be quick, for I can't wait—
My father Zeus expects me soon on high.'
With that he stuck two hands up, took the freight

Like one who'd lift a lorry to the sky;
Instantly pressure, by which I'd been gripped,
Abated, arms fell down like two dead flies;

I tottered over as both my feet slipped;*110*
But here dear Virgil caught me in my fall,
Whilst Dante witnessed, ironically clapped.

'How close, then, you were, forever to fail;
Saint Luke, his holy chapel not too far
Above where entry's to the hallowed portal;

And you to show your sentimental star
Would sacrifice it all—oh! Humankind,
Rife always to display weakness you are;

Only through death's purge can you change your mind.'
Though, then, his heavenly brightness briefly blinked*120*
As if taking stock of some deeper find—

The treasure to which the cosmos was linked
By threads invisible, yet wrought as steel
Or adamantine, strongest where it kinked—

His eyes looked up, and I felt it too ... real:
That dread returned that barely I can state
Of One whose hands were wounded, and his heel,

Who gambled Himself on divinity's fate;
For what if the sinless One had once sinned?
What then if the Son with the Father grates? *130*

Where goes then that Spirit of Love now shunned?
The cosmos falls apart, old Chaos reigns,
And all—with God Himself—wholly condemned?

But not so. He who lived—proving no stain—
Holding together all created order,
Avoiding the void that living's in vain,

Did more than any Herakles might shoulder—
Impressive, though, holding up the sky is:
Down, down He went where every being moulders,

Where arrogant, supreme and towering Dis *140*
Reigns, and who breaks his fatal, final spell?
I saw Him then, saw His name: Oh Christ!

My Lord, my God—whose eyes occupy hell
By right, by right rise up to living's light—
Except for Dis, then all, all will be well.

Thinking of Him, enduring Hell, Earth's night,
And lower still in those unspeakable bowels
Only my Dante ever painted right,

I trembled—for He is God of all rule.
Two things broke through my fevered reverie: *150*
For Virgil, seeing me in dumbstruck turmoil—

Concerned some fit of mad epilepsy
Would raze my senses more, reached down
To lift me up—save me—his constancy—

Though I myself had myself overthrown;
Yet now enfleshed, almost, and near the chapel,
The prize we all desired as most our own,

He, loving me as best as he was able,
Held me, and as he did a voice piped up,
One who already had triggered the trouble: *160*

Self-pitying, new querulous notes struck.
'You guys, what's up? What's taking you so long?
Come on—it's time for me to pass the buck—

That's how it works.' He paused, like some King Kong—
Majestic—the sky his, and his he grasped.
'I get the credit; afterwards, a gong,'

'Great once,' said Dante, 'but that moment's passed—
Setting a people free from Europe's yoke
Meant overleaping gates of Hell's impasse

To find a way for him only bespoke—*170*
Here purgatorial, heaven ahead;
But foolishly to turn to party jokes,

Then not applying what it means to lead—
To fall so short so near the sacred space
Is tragedy akin to being dead—

Who knows? Will he escape one day to face
That bliss Creation's self is groaning for?
Or will he cling—hopeless—to top-dog state,

Hoping in his supremacy for more?'
'I've held this long enough—your turn to do—*180*
I'm dizzy, eyes studying this wretched floor,

Whilst arms are occupied with this weight's blue.
We had agreement—don't welch on your debt—
And know, from here, you have fantastic views!'

Hardly a tempting pitch; more... desperate bet
That I again might reassume his load,
As millions had and millions would do yet

Come time to vote; for me, another road.
With politicians no more having truck:
No more believing narrow is what's broad. *190*

Already Dante had turned in disgust;
Now pointed to the path that led above;
But in our way, we saw their dead-end tracks

Of those embracing fear, discounting love,
Who'd swallowed whole the message of the mask—
Each one avoiding ... thereby to death driven!

Each lecturing each other about the task:
Be socially responsible, save the NHS.
So close they were, each talking from their arse;

So malodorous was the stench impressed$_{200}$
Upon me I scarce believed I'd left hell—
Their fear contagious in its emptiness.

Behind, I heard him scream—Herakles—
But now resolved no more to pity him—
Let God decide whether he had done well

Or rather caused countless deaths in time:
Along with masks I saw the needles pop
From arm to arm—to some it drew no harm,

But others floundered for steroids and ops;
Still more, their eyelids blinked, they stood a tick$_{210}$
And then a tock, then fatally they dropped.

And this proved our release—so many sick
And dying—the crowds in places thinned out,
So that the wall of solid human brick,

Impassable, showed a passageway straight through.
'Quick,' Dante said, 'if we're to go, go now.'
Angelic lightning in his limbs—he drew

Us past the labouring hospitalised crowds;
And there we were: before the higher step
Which led to a completely different show. *220*

Some grim smile broke Dante's face. 'Here it's steep
To climb: its poetry doesn't soar but seeps.'

CANTO 10: TOILETS

The Argument:

Leaving Herakles and making their way through the mask-wearing crowds, the pilgrims arrive at the ninth stair. There they find, each isolated and alone, three poets who have failed to make heaven for various reasons. These include two contemporary American poets and also John Wilmot, Earl of Rochester, the famous seventeenth century rake at the court of Charles II. Wilmot blesses the poet on his journey to heaven and asks that he be remembered there. Finally, they encounter one of the most famous poets of the twentieth century, Tom; but Tom is not alone. He is being interrogated by the greatest epic poet of the seventeenth century who has descended from heaven specially to do so. Dante joins in—and a ring Dante wears reveals a poet in Hell who unduly influenced Tom. Milton also wears a ring. Virgil is keen to move on and shares a cryptic message with the poet about the future of English poetry.

That still smile lightly gilding Dante's face—
His beautiful face—and with no humour lost
(Bemused by Purgatory's vatic embrace)

Quite baffled me; at least perplexed at first
As why he should regard this place so wry;
Or as some bee considers some flower most

Of all desirable when heaven's hive
Is mostly home much more to be desired;
But then I guess if heaven's where we live—

Unless one be a demon who's pariahed—10
One holds the presence of God always near:
All-where enjoying full notes of His lyre.

Whatever. The masked, blind crowds lost in fear
Were now long ways behind; new structures now
Infused this level's lonely atmosphere.

Ahead, apart, I saw in forlorn bowers—
Separate—weeping—wailing—unlit forms
With tight-knit concentration in their brows,

Reflecting passions whose vehement storms
Had put out light, though light of sorts arose—20
Too weak in all their thinking: savage, torn,

And yet, how they had tried—for that God knows;
So close to where the chapel of Saint Luke
Healed one as, clambering thorns, one finds the rose

At last, inhales its fragrance and is struck
With beauty so deep, the soul is mesmerised
And to retreat would be fatal, and to duck

Destiny. So, these bards—by the world eyed
So—seized the moment of their passing verse
Which almost lived, so close they were, but died ₃₀

Because some fault in technique, or much worse,
In them, meant that their Muse abandoned soul
As inspiration flagged on heaven's course.

The first, in some sequestered cubicle,
As if a ward all private—him alone—
I saw musing, posturing, precious, droll;

His words tapped out as typists might have done;
Admiring as he did withal his wit;
I put my ears forward—as to a phone—

To catch his composition, all of it: ₄₀
Starting with his signature, Aden Broncs,
Repeating—as would some moronic twit—

His name. Then to his business in 'Mohonk,
Sweet onus, Spring! How glad we are you're here,
As winter's been, we've waited so for yonks.

The ground of all fertility's been clear,
But now a poppy's popped up its pink head:
At rest our hearts with nothing now to fear.'

I couldn't help exclaim, 'This verse seems dead,
Monotonous,' and Dante straight agreed, 50
Whilst Virgil wanted something else to read!

The rhyming just to rhyming seemed to lead,
And, furthermore, the meter's plodding beat
Induced a sleep-like, catatonic need.

But hearing my remark, Aden made bleat:
'I can do feminine rhymes too, ya' know.'
And thereby aroused, he sat up in his seat,

Began some verses that I couldn't follow,
But the point was, he managed to rhyme 'crises'—
Semantics all gone, and content all hollow— 60

Yet joy in him to reach the clinch word, 'Pisces'.
Expecting our applause—but silence trailed
As when not sixes, two ones on two dice

Appear—which means his rhyming gamble's failed.
We moved away. 'He'll make Saint Luke's at last,'
Said Dante. 'For him too our Lord was nailed.'

We paused, reflecting on our own dark pasts,
Virgil and I, and how the Great One came
Down to experience all death's vile taste,

And thinking so revived—thinking His name— 70
That tremor of awe one could not control,
So that our bodies shook, fearful of Him;

But shaking felt fresh purging of our souls,
Till, breaking the spell that 'nail' had induced,
I wittered with a question why Bronc stalled

Just short of healing, so near to Saint Luke's;
Believing, as he did, what held him back?
'Alas,' said Dante, 'lack of joy's real juice

That marks every Christian who's on Christ's true track:
What point repeating creeds, or bowing knees,$_{80}$
Or airy signs of crosses and knick-knacks,

If harboured in's a bitter devotee?
A carping mind that's restless to accuse,
And one attacking all real poetry?

He turned, for we had no time more to lose.
Yet scarce had moved a foot when, lo! Behold!
We stumbled on a sad, solitary booth,

So out of keeping—with its unique mould;
Its composition seemed to be a shrine—
Quite ludicrous design—quite over-bold:$_{90}$

Whose outside lettering blared, 'Poetry's mine'.
In smaller type: 'Worship my genius',
Then smaller still: 'My works are sheer divine.'

Yet vaunting done, and incandescent puff
Aside, something—a sound—gave evidence
That all was not right: such weeping, groans—proof.

I looked inside—within, a barest tent,
Furnished with baubles, bits of Latin, Greek,
And poor Zeke there, his mind now overbent

With learning—scraps, of which old French was peak— *100*
And maybe in arrangements to be found
He'd write the sonnets Shakespeare wrote, unique.

I pitied him there, listless legs aground,
And praying, sorrow's cloth upon his head,
The while his muse hovered close, circled round:

Dear God—to not be found among the dead!
Who'd not be moved to hear such desperate songs?
'His songs can soar, but a fly-fishers' lead

Is how his heart sinks,' said Dante, 'So wrong,
For all the Hail Mary's he has performed. *110*
So now he stays here, for who knows how long?

For all the put-downs—for which he squirms—
Of others, now he pays a fuller penance,
For here is where exhausted falsehood turns

To meet its truth, and can no more advance—
Like some high tide that covers all the beach,
Till last the Moon pulls back its arrogance:

We see the derelict shore that once preached
Its fullness in waves of such short duration,
Now stranded, strewn with everything light's bleached. *120*

Such is our human achievement, creation;
But rest assured, beyond Saint Luke's the promise
He made—who cannot be forsworn—is waiting.'

Impatient I, that Dante's discourse finish,
Stepping into his tent, accosting Zeke,
Disrupting prayers he thought his own office,

As if to God he qualified to speak
Alone, more accurately had ears to hear;
And yet, to see him there, pathetic, weak—

Where was the Yahweh Moses heard, and feared? $_{130}$
Where vigour, vim that led from Egypt out?
Heart that held fast one hundred and twenty years?

I said—as best I could—as words allowed—
'Greetings my brother, do you prophesy?
Are your words ones that heaven too's espoused?

What Muse lives in you now, or does light die?'
Slowly, reluctantly, he turned from prayer.
Noticed—his hands, a well-thumbed rosary,

As if planed by effort till it was bare
Of all distinction a wooden bead had— $_{140}$
Might have in its God-given signature.

So strange the look he gave me, slightly mad,
Beside himself, or in some kind of panic,
But slo-moed—like prayers held back a tad

His vehemence. 'Ha! You!' he said, 'Satanic:
Up from that HellWard, grime upon your face;
I am not fooled: my name is Zeke Jock Manic

Whose sonnets the world will read, love, embrace,
For heaven and earth have both set their seal;
As you see me now—in a state of grace!' *150*

If a blessed spirit could let anger feel
Then Dante felt just that now—hues of red
Suffused his form, and yet heaven's control

Through grace kept Dante straight, to the point led:
'The One decides whose works live and whose not;
Who arbitrates the heart—discerning greed

From others marked by mercy, heaven's lot.
Stand, then, abashed, confessing all your sin,
Then chance, heaven relents, allows your shot.'

How strange it was: the turmoil Zeke was in, *160*
Almost it seemed against an inner will,
He stood to summon that real truth within.

'Mary,' he said, 'ever my angel still—
Her intercession may my misspoke cover.'
Then, 'I covet every man's scope and skill!'

Abrupt and blunt, and his pretence all over.
I saw with my own eyes, Dante's hand rise up
And with one motion embrace him as brother.

'His mother too,' he said, 'drank from that cup
He drank from; keep that in mind as the first$_{170}$
Principle, if you are to reach the top

Of this steep climb—He only quenches thirst,
Is food enough for all ravenous spirits.
The table's spread—bless be those, those the worst

Even, yet through His sacrifice inherit
His kingdom.' Subdued, trembling on his knees,
Zeke prayed, 'One line of mine may find His merit

In that kingdom He has founded, if He please.'
Again, but softly, lips began to move;
I heard mention of saints, Saint Peter's keys,$_{180}$

But not Saint Luke's, the way we had to strive.
Leaving him, then, praying for his new way,
We crossed to where another sought to live:

A line stretched back to lost and ancient days;
We marked its course and followed on its trail;
Methought my host excited in his praise

Of one whose whole short life had been to fail,
Except at that one moment nearing death
When Mary and mercy were both revealed:

'Upwards in a storm wind, light as a leaf,$_{190}$
(I interviewed Buonconte on the Mount)
It's truth I speak—in heaven he's released;

One tear saved him; how many years to count?
Some seven hundred; this one, half of that—
Still labouring for release, John Wilmot,

Lord Rochester: unbelief's great poet.'
There, in a corner, edged to one side,
Rochester mouthed his ambivalent state:

'Worst part of me and hated far and wide,
Through all the town a common fucking post$_{200}$
On whom each whore's cunt can greasily slide ...

And yet, did not your mother love you most;
Your wife pray to God with furious intent
To save your soul and bring you home at last?

These women, then, not whores in pleasures spent,
But dames who moved you nearer more to God,
Oblivious of sacrifice's expense.'

He turned from murmuring his bits and bobs;
'My life, my body, all was pissing matter;
Bladder broken, unfit to do its job,$_{210}$

Like my whole life, each word I came to utter...'
His voice trailed off, as dirty water does,
Till finally it weeps into a gutter.

So down, defeated, in his shabby clothes,
Not royal lord who stood before his king;
I felt such pity, how he'd come to loathe

Himself. But then, something so surprising:
He asked me to read him a special passage.
'For me,' he said, his eyes alight, imploring.

His sudden brightness transformed his dark image, _220_
As if a dead torch's battery gave shine,
So, through its light, we saw a new message.

Then Dante handed me the Book divine.
I opened up the page of Fifty-Three
And read to him exactly every line:

'Who will believe? Who knows His mystery?
From the dry ground—without that comeliness
Attending all desire, all works of beauty;

Inheriting not mankind's more but less;
Despised, rejected, acquainted with grief— _230_
His way—that way of cross—that's bruised, oppressed,

Inconsequential as a falling leaf,
Sheep-dumb, and dumber sheep damned to the slaughter;
Who threatened no words, nor voiced no relief.

His life given for each lost son, dear daughter;
Oh! Such a One as He is, even dead—
No maggot on his corpse, master of matter;

Then hear the cry of one, destruction-bred,
Beside His cross, upon the cross his own,
"Remember me in your kingdom," he said. _240_

Today with me, in paradise your home,
You will be with Me.' How Rochester sobbed
Unbearable to the point of his break-down:

All that he owed God and from God had robbed.
But now as his confession reached its low,
I saw the stirrings of his loathing stopped—

New grace, like some new galaxy formed, glowed—
His body lifted, and at its heart, his heart
Began to be a spirit Christ's own showed.

Though dead as dead bones—yet through Him life
    starts:$_{250}$
In vast valleys those dead might live again
Whole, from those billion, billion, broken shards.

'Master,' I said, 'Of lustings in lost veins;
Abashed I am to say I loved your works,
Inspired by filth that ought induce deep shame;

How cutting, though, your lines no horrors shirked,
Precise in all the vitriol and vile
Whose depths suggested some foundation lurked

Beyond, unlike accumulated evils
Depicted in your verse. Which leads you here:$_{260}$
God's StairWell where we both find life and live.'

He smiled, the first time, as from ear to ear.
'You go,' he said, 'disciple of strange sorts;
Excel me, do more: and as you draw near

To that high place from where I'm falling short,
Remember me to Him who was despised—
Through Him my brazen horns will be gold wrought;

There is a crown for those that He has raised;
Let all my works be dust, so this one thing:
Together, at the end, we be with Christ.'₂₇₀

He shuddered at those thoughts salvation brings:
The hope the whole creation's yearning for—
At last, to see His beauty, full and limning,

As holy haloes might existence's store,
If visible or not. How glorious
That One whose presence leaves us wanting more,

Whose Being not only creates, sustains us,
But here with Rochester redeems—within
Him now, I sensed the glory, dead the lust.

But Dante touched my arm. 'Forget those sins,'₂₈₀
He said. 'Your friend Wilmot will find his way;
Best not to brood what was amiss, let in

Stray thoughts that straggle and lead more astray.
Perhaps he'll join us at Saint Luke's—but we
Must get there before ending of your day.'

Reluctant to leave such a one as he,
Yet knowing Dante knew better and best;
Besides, was also king of true poetry;

With Virgil, then, we quit; we'd had our rest,
And now the final passage on this stair 290
Awaited us—a poet with no nest,

Restless in extreme and being not there,
Macavity-like, always half-way in
That other world or invisible sphere

Which most deny, so compounding their sin;
Not he. Oh! How his suffering's entrenched
With all the indecision marring men.

Even daring to eat a peach seemed to wrench
His mind in convolutions unspeakable;
Or think of she who died elsewhere—a wench 300

Committing fornication—at least able
So to do, not paralysed from waist down
(Unlike Wilmot who there proved so capable).

But Tom now ruminated not alone:
Beside him, austere and gaunt, that giant
Who dwarfed all English poets with his tome,

All shining, light glorious and triumphant.
I gasped—my knees buckled—to see him so:
Lecturing Tom as if watering a plant!

Before my words could leave my throat and go 310
To the temple in his ear, Dante said, 'John—
Hail great master of English iambic flow!

I see from heaven, and for this stalled son
You've come.' Then Milton turned, his face a flame,
Like some phalanx of fiery power that stuns

Merely to see. But what he saw—the name
Of Dante standing upright before him.
'Why praise me so, you know my verse seems lame

Beside your own—your heaven truly climbs,
But mine seems not so realised, precise?'₃₂₀
He paused—both laughed—embraced heavenly limbs

In joy at this unexpected surprise:
Meeting so thus. It seemed then, as they did,
No membrane, joint or limb, exclusive bars,

Obscured their mutual love or caused it hid;
Rather, in that instant all soul in soul
Was open, pure and naked, yet still clad!

Wonder to behold, and not in this world
Possible. But soon as done it was over,
As purposes for us resumed control.₃₃₀

Oh! How I wished I too was such a lover,
Could within me give so much to someone;
And I thought of her: my beautiful other ...

But then I heard the stern censorious tone
Of Milton dig down in Tom's blighted root:
'What kind of line is "April's cruellest month"?

Why do you blacken life and make it soot?
How can you think to join great Dante in
That paradise where you eat living fruit

When you are lost so far and so alone?'*340*
Here Dante chipped in too: 'Those women wait,
Still wait, and not for you to signal groans

Of self-pity, or that it is 'Too late',
As if love had limits bounded by our time,
Or with the body knew a sell-by-date.

What folly—like, your self-conscious rhymes,
And lack thereof. You had the models, sure,
Why even Virgil's here—study his lines!

But you? Listening to Ezra Pound's obscure,
Unsettled, and frankly crazy agitations,*350*
Posing as advice—floundering on his shore!

You know where he is now: at his lost station
Below where HellWard traps unwary pride,
Those guilty of literary depredations.

See here.' He raised his left hand from his side;
His index finger wore a ruby ring,
Which seemed so small at first, but then grew wide,

Enlarged as a screen that Tom was studying,
Intent, and the while his face pierced with pain;
Upsurging from below was Ezra's sting:*360*

142

Those incoherent languages that strained—
Like ancient Greek or Chinese hieroglyphics—
To be as English verse, but strained in vain,

For all his hyperbole, ego-tricks
That master self-publicist mustered well—
Yet Museless—what else? All proves soporific.

Some image of Pound in his ward of Hell
Filtered up like rising cigarette smoke,
Only not silent but in deafening peals

Of languages no-one wanted or spoke: _370_
Fumes deadened, yet aggravated the while.
'I see,' said Tom in tears. 'Ezra's a joke?'

'Yes, one the world's followed many a mile
And not because any thought his work good,
Or that his mixing languages had style;

Oh no!' said Dante, 'the reasons are mad:
Like Nimrod building his own Babel, Pound
Sought deity in making poetry bad;

To be a god beyond Apollo's bound
Of metrics—what true English is about; _380_
He stamped your faces hard into the ground

With his fascistic, imperial boot;
Sans structure, beauty, form or even line;
And to say my work—mine!—is at his root!'

143

Here Milton chuckled: 'Your heavenly design
Besides his diarrhoea and verbal crimes?
For every literal in Hell he's fined,

No way out! Modernism's had its time;
But you, Tom, now see my sapphire ring:
Its matching sky-blue shows the cosmos rhymes.' 390

With that, he raised his right index finger
And its glorious ring incandescent—
Light pointing skyward to heaven's high hangar

There. So that blue with other colours blent,
As if the sky had become a huge screen
And on it one image of what life meant—

At least for Tom: what life for him should mean.
I caught a glimpse in that magic of V—
His wife—whose love had washed him clean

Eventually. Beyond this Purgatory—400
The StairWell we were at—she beckoned, prayed;
And Tom could see his own Divine Lady,

The help-meet God at the beginning made:
Through the woman, then, salvation comes.
Tom's face lit with joy; his past pain erased.

Time coming when his purgatory was done.
But I myself could not stop other thoughts
Rioting, thinking of that Lady, one

Who'd loved me even though I'd fallen short.
Where was she now? Perhaps an echo heard$_{410}$
As V beckoned Tom—still small voice I caught

Also encouraging me to move upwards,
No more delay. I sensed that Virgil too,
Fed up with Modernism's dark absurd

Wanted to renew the climb—there's more to do.
Was it his hand I felt clasp mine to lead
Away? I turned. He winked as schemers do.

'A third ring must be found,' his whisper said,
'If English poetry shall rise from the dead.'

CANTO 11: AIR LIGHT

The Argument:

The poet is bemused by the rings of poetry that the pilgrim has seen on Milton and Dante's fingers, so Dante now explains how he came to acquire his ring. Through it, the pilgrim glimpses the cosmic task ahead for Dante in God's enormous plan. They reach the tenth stair and find there a lonely philosopher who spent his life denying God until, looking at the evidence, he changed his mind and published a book about his revised views. Erstwhile colleagues and friends condemned him for his theism, but he held fast to his belief. On leaving him, they suddenly encounter the end of the StairWell and a ladder spanning the abyss where they can see a DoorWay ahead. Balanced midway across the ladder is another famous philosopher. He boasts about what he has achieved, and pursues his way across, although seemingly never getting any nearer as the group close the distance between him and them. In jealous rage he claims his preeminence. Suddenly, as with Job, the Divine Presence asks him

three questions; his failure to answer the third one has dire consequences. But the group arrive at the door of the DoorWay—a door
with no handle and no lock.

Dazed, (by those words that Virgil spoke before
About another potent ring—third one—
That only poets who drew the Muse's power,

And worshipped, on His unassailable throne,
Him—One whose name could conjure existence
Into being, and all perfectly done)

I staggered forward, not knowing the whence
Or why—so besotted by my jewelled thoughts,
Like diamonds unfazed by mere common sense,

Sparkling in the pride of light their forms caught. 10
Until at last to break through reveries
I fantasised, Dante pulled me up short:

'The ring I wear is one of great poetry,
Gifted to me by that One whom I serve,
And through Apollo in the highest skies;

To the sublime commit; and not to swerve
Must be your plan—intention—heart's desire,
So that in rising never lose your nerve;

Do not falter before the healing's fire
In that chapel where Luke will be your purge; 20
Besides', he said—attention on the wire,

147

Curiosity's overwhelming urge
To know more—'this ring has in it my name,
My real name, and its full creative charge—

Who I really am—as on a white stone
Subsumed within this glowing ruby red.'
With that his hand appeared with the ring on;

Now not delving into the lower depths
Where Pound was, but radiating up—out—
Around—towards me—its profound effects$_{30}$

Vibrating through like that army's great shout
Which brought down town and walls of Jericho.
So, my whole being, knocked out by its clout,

Entered another space I had to go:
I saw the Twins, fifty or so light years
From Earth, Medusa Nebula's faint glow,

And there—therein—Dante's ring my mind steered
To see the great work he had yet to do:
Seed gases, vapours, bring to birth new stars,

New planets, worlds that God planned, allowed$_{40}$
In that new order that was soon to be;
A glimpse—a hint—what Dante followed through—

Amazed, by glory and complexity
Alike, out of my body, then back in,
I woke, and his ring could no longer see;

But still inspired by all I had just seen
In that millisecond's momentary flash
Containing a million years of God's dream!

I yearned to be part of that order's cache:
New world, not like the old, corrupted, done $_{50}$
For; no—free of hypocrisy, death and trash.

Now Dante smiled—my thoughts he read along,
As one might read a laptop's screen and laugh:
My scrunched-up words so short of forming songs.

'Perhaps in heaven, if you push hard enough,
And He for whom nothing's too difficult
Grant you a ring that you will wield with strength.'

I wondered at his world—and its occult
Mysteries, powers, exultations, lights,
Abundantly possessed—yet not to vaunt— $_{60}$

His poetry magnified to new heights
Where stars themselves would constellate, align
In terza rima on space's threadbare weight;

And how those stars hung—impossible signs
Of glories greater than imagined now—
All pointing too to One's faultless design.

But move we must—Saint Luke's beckoned above,
And what was in Paradise or that Heaven
Beyond and through the DoorWay into love

Would sure astonish more than red rings even,₇₀
If we could but make this before I died.
A while I stood, a-wanting to be shriven,

And praying in my soul to quell my pride—
That Lord of all glory to hear my prayer—
To rid my tongue-filled verse of all that's lied,

Or lying so, Dante-like, get to 'there'
Where all the rainbow colours show as one:
More flawless than driven-snow, and more pure.

But then ahead I saw where one had gone
Before, attempting to make sense of it;₈₀
For all that mind might make—intellect spawn—

There, higgledy-piggledy, as bat wings flit
As dark descends and the whole world turns black,
So, in this corner, weak ideas just lit

Enough light to save mind from its own rack.
'Thank God you've come,' the sad, lone sophist said.
'You know where I have been; I can't go back.'

His voice was ripped with terror's cutting blade,
Though I had no notion of who he was
Or where he'd been. 'Tell me, your name, your trade,₉₀

And how from HellWard you escaped its paws—
Mouse-like—squeaking in a night that doesn't come
Here'; and his rapid high-pitched gabble paused,

As one weighing how best describe his doom.
At last, he spoke, each word clear, deliberate;
Which turned his corner—more light—to a room

Enlarging who he was—at any rate:
'Professor A.I. Flight, and for many years
World class philosopher, hero of debate;

Why, I critiqued Lewis without fear,*100*
Made atheism mainstream—default belief—
Encouraged humanists to mock and cheer

With confidence: where's God and where's the beef
That proves He ever existed at all?
My scepticism was my fun, my mischief.'

But as he said those words, misgiving's thrall
Held him in its vice-like, unforgiving grip:
Dark tears ran down his cheeks like acid's spoil.

He struggled for more words as infirm lips
Quivered. 'I lost it at the end, you know.'*110*
His eyes pleaded. 'Dementia, knowledge stripped

From me and with it my high pride brought low;
Ah!' An anguished outburst from his deep soul.
'Destined and doomed,' he cried, 'to hell to go!

But, but ...' almost now he could not control
That depth of feeling wracking what mind held
In memory still but could not reach, unfold.

So Dante, with his ring—and what it spelled—
Reached out his hand to still Flight's sorry tremblings
Caused by that darkness in which Flight's thoughts
    gelled—*120*

Stuck fly-like in jelly's stationary fumblings;
And as he did, his ring glowed and light burst
Forth: halo—enveloping, unencumbering

Flight from that illness with which he was cursed.
A surge of joy—sudden—lit his whole face.
'My mind is back—my life has been a verse—

Like poetry, yet bad, meter displaced;
But this one thing my great God recognised
In me—let me see in His sacred space:

Remember—I saw through in time the lies: *130*
Telling them straight where the evidence went—
Nothing explained from matter how came life?

There had to be a God—a deep intent
Or order that made all things possible;
Impossible that chance willed to invent

A universe where such beauty's visible;
And too, where what is truly real, is not!'
He paused, quite overwhelmed—how long the fool

He'd played, but more: immensity, the lot;
Who could comprehend such reality—*140*
Its scale, involvedness, and how begot?

'And for my pains, godless jackals racked me—
Savage as beasts—who erstwhile were colleagues,
Because I stood for truth's fidelity.

Their former loyalties not worth a fig;
Such be those secular fools who hate God.
What matter? Spewage, troughing like pigs,

I took my leave and left one book of good,
Enraging them further: called me 'senile'—
They did!—'demented', any words to prod $_{150}$

Me to revoke the truth that made me smile
And why now I am here! Though suffering
To be with God, which from here's a long mile,

But I see His cosmos through Dante's ring,
Brought here now for solace.' With that he ceased.
He had defended the Right—that some Thing—

No!—some Mind made order's masterpiece:
This cosmos, one and only universe;
Why speculate or gabble like geese—

There are a million planets like the Earth, $_{160}$
That multi-verses really do exist,
Evidence for which is all a turd's worth?

He held the truth, though not accepting Christ,
So lapsed into a silence he'd long hold,
On StairWell till God recalled him home, blessed.

How long to wait before God's arms enfold
Him once more? How long mind argue himself:
From thinking to grace in that higher world?

But Dante heard my thoughts and knew the gulf
Between this StairWell here and DoorWay next, *170*
And sighed. 'Yes, blessed, but still from God aloof

Until released, allowed to make that step
That leads to faultless life and no mistake,
That fullness which being close to God gets.'

He paused. All clear to him and no mistake,
No possibility ever to err,
For suffering plainly no more, no mistake,

Foregone for His suffering's sake. So here
We were, still in that vale where visibly
All was not purged—so high, and yet nowhere. *180*

What did they matter, these dim philosophies
And speculations of minds led astray,
Leading so many others too to lies?

How bridge the gap, how find the true DoorWay
To that sphere where the immortal One walked
And not the least angel wanted to stray?

Now Virgil gasped, as one who being stalked—
But unaware—turns, sees the beast behind,
Only front-on, looming a ladder baulked,

Blocking our path ahead, rendering blind *190*
Our sight to all else bar the chasm it bridged
In glorious confidence as it shined.

Around it, wreathing, dancing angels arched
Above, beneath, so perfect in their light;
Though one small human form seemed to be perched

Midway across the span of mind's deep height.
Midway—so close, then, to that other side
Where perhaps a door led to all delight?

But whatever, wavering midway in pride,
He waved to us whilst tottering this way, *200*
Then that—I feared for him, feared he would slide—

Go over into abyss, should he stray.
Who was this 'Blondin' on Niagara Falls?
What was the pit beneath that knew no day?

I peered and instantly had to recoil—
I knew the place—myself had been there too:
Below the ladder 'Blondin' scaled was Hell.

Now Dante urged me on—what I must do;
And not alone, as Virgil blanched, bleached white:
To follow 'Blondin'—courage from us flew. *210*

'Who is the man out there—unafraid quite—
Ignoring even angels and their forms
Of beauty—why this ladder hung on night?

How go back now? What? To Hell to return?
It cannot be! 'Behold,' said Dante, boldly,
'For Jacob's Ladder bridges these two zones—

See how its base rests on one stone that's holding
Its whole structure up; one stone, as the Old
Has it, or one rock the New, is unfolding

Continually—dreaming its end is gold—$_{220}$
Fulfilment of prophecies long ago:
In dreams every truth is told, foretold,

At Bethel Jacob knew the God who knows.'
But then, at this point, a voice from the midst,
Who flapping hard to hold—as might a crow—

Midway suspended, croaked out in vain angst:
'My name's Professor I.M. Air, nearly there—
Philosophy cuts through lies that work against

All human happiness—just look how far
I've come. My great book: Language Lies and Liquids—$_{230}$
A best-seller in sixty-six different versions

By which I verify—I meant, get rid
Of—any statement claiming 'otherness',
Through classifying them as simply stupid;

Great trick, and how it worked! Made God seem less—
Religion superstitious—Hume would be proud:
All knowledge—always known—is now a guess;

It unbecomes—I cry, "Bingo!" out loud,
For I'm an Oxonian—we chuckle—discreet—
With certain triumphs that must be allowed.'$_{240}$

But then he paused as in his mind he met
Another memory that de-confirmed
The self-satisfactions he'd found so sweet.

'Pneumonia first, in a New York term,
Became indicative I neared my end;
All part of natural process, no concern;

Only I entered a different tent—
An Other realm where living's not like here;
I came back—an NDE's where I went.

I said, I thought what I believed was queer;$_{250}$
Revision needed—what was that Red Light
Who, whichever way I turned, still stayed near?

Surely, something beyond death held on tight
And I was privileged to be so held;
And yet, and yet—to hell with all His shite:

Humanist, first and foremost I am spelled—
Imagine their disappointment in me—
Recanting atheism, saying it's shelved,

Because one coma and its reveries,
(Which intellectually I could not deny)$_{260}$
Meant me debarred from secular committees?

Me excommunicate? Lose friends? For why?
Some silly warning in four-minute's death?
You see me now? I climb—and look, how high!'

I stood beside the stone and took a breath—
Across the ladder and beyond mid-way,
Closer he rose to the peak's spectral wreath—

Like smoke on Mount Sinai obscuring day,
As well as what that summit held in store
And there what message Moses must obey! $_{270}$

Almost distracted—was there there a door
Behind the wreath and on the other side?
But Dante sharply said, 'We're not tourists here.'

I had to step out; but so deep, so wide
The canyon Air was now three parts across;
Yet faith meant going could not be denied—

To stay—a hypocrite to live with loss.
Fond Virgil squeezed my arm to give support,
Like me, he too dreaded treading this fosse.

But there we were, three on the ladder's cart $_{280}$
To carry us—we hoped—to Paradise,
Or at least the Doorway where heaven starts.

How sweet those angels and their exercise,
As circling, beguiling us ever on,
My mind gained strength, not just seeing their lithe

Limbs—hearing harmonic notes, subtle tunes,
That filled the soul within with confidence;
Almost I barely looked or thought of 'down'—

Below my feet no hell could touch my sense.
I first in queue and Dante at the rear; *290*
We seemed to gain in time on Air's advance,

So that, though he no closer, we were near.
He turned and saw us closing and his face
Blotched red with fury, lips began to sweat:

'O what the fuck, then? This is all my space!
I'm THE philosopher, better than Hume;
I was here first—and you can't take my place.'

How weird his logic's emotional loom.
But one thing sure: him there, we could not pass,
Were stuck above Hell till he gave us room. *300*

So far we'd come, and yet ahead this loss:
Some Prince of Air who barred our pathway hence
For reasons personal, ambitious, crass.

But then three things, unlike before or since
I'd ever witnessed, simultaneously stirred:
I felt an ill wind from below up-rinse

Our bodies as its malevolence lured
Souls downwards, clasping with its gelid grip;
Cocytus—frozen river—voices heard—

Awoken, his power called us for a dip $_{310}$
Below! Jacob's Ladder on which we stood
Began to ripple as if it were rope

Lassoing out to shake off or include
I could not say, but my heart froze with fear
And spittle in my throat became imbued

With such a hardness that it was stuck there;
I wrestled to swallow and all the while
It throbbed, and then I knew: He ...He was here!

Effortless—as before for His disciples—
Now through the door, I saw His glorious light: $_{320}$
Resting my knees on rungs—unworthy, vile—

Too sensing Virgil bowed before the sight.
At first, a Voice mellifluous as bees
And just as soft, though rising to stern heights,

Addressed Himself to one not bending knees.
'Answer me, Philosopher, if you can,
Who's come so far through rationality,

Perhaps, to pave the way for every man
To find My paradise behind these doors;
Just three questions, so not hard for you then?' $_{330}$

'Was that question first?' Air mocked, sought to score,
But as a spider feels throughout his web
Each tiny movement and each minute tremor,

So, I felt Air's confidence lacked all legs.
'Where were you when I laid the earth's foundation,
Its bases put in place, held it with pegs?'

He paused—as Air too reviewed his education.
At last: 'The question makes no sense,' he said,
'There's no empirical verification.'

'When did you walk on the deep ocean's bed?'$_{340}$
'Preposterous!' Air retorted in an instant,
'These questions won't do—they're not Tripos led.'

But now the Voice assumed another slant,
Deeper, darker and with ominous threat:
'And are the gates of death in your command?'

He wavered, I felt it: the redness, the sweat
When under heat, and knowing bees could sting,
And harmony itself become tuneless death.

'I ... I ... I' but no words formed—sound could sing—
Except the blast beneath rose up, with Air$_{350}$
Standing, so fully exposed to its shattering

Cold, whilst we huddled in worship and prayer.
One cry, one solitary and last cry
And Air to Cocytus fell like a meteor,

Down to the place of deepest treachery—
Reason betrayed, for letting meaning fray;
I could not help myself—opened one eye

To peek and see the downward spirals made
Through rapid descent scraping such sharp sparks
As gravity against the upward blast played; *360*

The fiery furnace of his mental arts
Meeting such ice as will not ever melt—
But not his mind is caught, but his cold heart.

At last, a speck, consumed in ice's tumult,
Air disappeared. The deathly breath reined back,
A sort of calm reigned, brought fear to a halt.

Collectively, we stood, though dazed and racked;
So, Virgil, I, at least; though Dante's eyes
Were fixed in rapture where the door was hacked;

Plain, visible now, and no more sophistries. *370*
How Dante yearned to see his Master more;
But now the task was getting us to rise,

Press on—there it was, ahead, that great Door.
Regaining balance on our slender thread,
We pushed onwards: the prize worth suffering for.

But round and round, like some fly in my head,
I kept asking, How had Air fallen so?
So close to living, now so lost, so dead?

We reached the Door and saw a ledge below
On which to stand. Dismounting, there we stood, *380*
And clueless, I looked on, then what to do?

No handle—lock—defaced the frame of wood—
Showed means by which we'd enter in; all smooth
Its surface was, as if it had been scrubbed

Then varnished, polished with the shine of truth,
Save in the top right corner of the frame
I saw a sign I scarce could scan, peruse:

But as I struggled, so in view my name
As Scorpio's sign appeared, abstruse, arcane.

CANTO 12: ST LUKE'S CHAPEL

T he Argument:

At the door with no handle, lock, or key, and with Dante disappeared, Virgil and the pilgrim seem in a hopeless situation. But the pilgrim remembers a text that Virgil could not have known, and in implementing its advice suddenly stumbles through the door; only to find himself back on the operating table where his cancer is about to be removed. His surgeon is St Luke, the Ox, the sign of Taurus, the pilgrim's opposite and so nemesis. However, at the point of maximum despair, the lovely Lady Linda appears and holds the pilgrim's hand through the cutting operation. The Lady works her art and staunches the bleeding, and painting his finger a bright ring consolidates itself. She disappears to the pilgrim's grief, but he walks with St Luke into the garden, sees the ducks, and looks into the pond. There he is drawn into a vision in which an eye also sees him. The Lovely Lady fleetingly appears: how can the pilgrim reach her? St Luke advises him.

I turned my head to see him there; and there
He was, but Dante'd disappeared—alone
We were on that great ledge, and stuck before

Some door that lacked a logic of its own:
No handle, lock or key to enter in,
And no way back; the ladder now had gone.

We seemed suspended on one empty nothing!
I saw in Virgil's face more fear than slight;
Along with me, consider where we'd been,

So much ascending to reach beyond night—*10*
Was this the end, a final comfort then?
Life a lost island, stranded in no light?

His eyes implored—me to make amends?
As if I could, as if I'd some sneak phrase
Which uttered would burst this DoorWay open?

But what I had, came back from earlier days:
Memories, texts, promises from the Word;
Ones Virgil never knew, studied their lays.

'I think,' I said, 'if what be true is heard
And acted on, we knock—with our hearts bare—*20*
Three times and He who always listens ... stirs!

Bewildered, he gave me a vacant stare;
But there was no time to lose, and so I knocked,
Three times, as hard as my weak heart would dare.

Then, suddenly, as if stumbling half-cocked,
Through the DoorWay my whole being shuffled forth—
To where my whole fate could not be unlocked:

I looked—amazed—and with revulsion's froth;
There, on that operating table lay ...
Myself! Above me, a surgeon in mask—30

As Jesus to his disciples those days
Appearing when all the doors were shut firm,
They worshipping Him with resurrection's praise;

But me—got through—but more like a trapped worm
Under examination's probing spear;
Above the mask, the ceiling's circling turn,

Like I'd been drugged—but not Earth, heaven's sphere
Spun round inside my head, and what I saw
Was indistinct light, sparks, most surely, stars;

A pattern forming, the Crab Nebula,40
The Pleiades, and then the give-away:
Bright Aldebaran, light years off and far,

But all within the band that Taurus plays.
One-eight-o degrees my time had gone back:
Back to the hospital and those sick days,

To cancer and all my sarcoma's sick.
'This should not be,' I gasped, despairing breath,
'My glyph's the Scorpion, not Taurus' clique,

Which opposite's my adverse point of death.'
Then looking up the surgeon who bent over,$_{50}$
Stripped off his mask—as if some facile sheath—

Revealing an ox's head the sheath had covered.
Again, I gasped, aghast, repulsed, repelled;
But his voice said, 'I'm Luke and I'm your lover!'

With that the spear—or scalpel?—that he held
Plunged down into deepest depths of my gut,
Excising in me what would never yield:

Tumour and ego, yes, and all the slut
Thoughts that comprised my life wholly to date.
I shivered fearful as a dying brute$_{60}$

Who knows the hunter's spear will seal his fate.
But just then, just when I'd given up hope,
Resigned to all of hell's dazzling, dark shapes,

I felt a hand touch mine as could elope
My being to altered time—other space—
Provide—for all my falling—a new rope

To hold me up: the softness of her face
Made my eyes turn and see her blue, blue eyes
And in them all the mercy love could trace.

'My Lady Linda!' I said, full surprised.$_{70}$
'You've come for me—is there then a way out?'
She nodded blissfully, squeezed my hand tight.

'You are with Saint Luke—with him is no doubt.'
I felt his spear working within, my blood
Begin to spill, some dark evil uproot.

In my mind's eye it seemed pointless, no good;
No implement could dig down deep enough—
Evil was in me like grain in the wood:

However planed back, always more bad stuff,
And if Luke cut too much then what would be?$_{80}$
No blood in me and there'd be no life left.

'My hand,' she said, 'take it and stay with me.'
The softness of her sweet voice hypnotised;
Dream-like she led me in my revery:

The Chapel of Saint Luke—as curtains prised
Open with swish of her commanding arms—
Suddenly hove into view without disguise:

Most wondrous, not just the crucifix's balm
Raised high above the altar of her works,
But studio where her art healed all harm$_{90}$

Through palettes of colours' intensest arcs.
One hand, I saw, manipulate a brush
In crimson paint dipping to do its task.

So slowly, then, exact and with no rush—
Her lovely hand began to paint its form:
So delicate each stroke, each minute splash

Following precisely the spear's slashed seam,
And as each droplet dripped its signature—
Its autograph of love—so my blood, keen

To flow, was stilled by her art's overture. *100*
I felt the pain abate; I heard Saint Luke
Talk to my love and talk of being 'sure'.

The spear was gone; the wound a lasting fluke;
But now I had to get up—get up—go;
But to do so—the energy it took!

I could barely move—even thinking slow
And slower. How steer through the Chapel proper,
Breakthrough where spirits, unimpeded, flow?

'Dearest,' I cried, 'Your man's as one on fly-paper;
I cannot move—all my engines inside, *110*
My brain itself is in this desperate torpor!

Help me!' I sensed her restless by my side;
The brush she'd used to stitch my wound put down,
Another taken, soon to be applied.

She dipped its tip in paint of golden-brown,
Rich as brown earth, and bright as heaven's gold;
That finger of my left hand held as her own.

Meticulous—brush around my finger rolled;
Once, twice and thrice the tickling paint's firm stick
Adhered to human flesh, wholly involved— *120*

What was the paint—how far in did it reach?
But scarcely had I time to think too much
When her voice—altered in patterns of speech—

Spoke as her mother might, or other vouched:
'Apollo grants this gift to you—in love.'
With that, that finger lifted and her lips touched,

And in my total being my soul moved.
I stood as one who'd never stood before—
Released—one as innocent as a dove.

So confident: ahead could see the Door,*130*
That Door that truly led to Paradise.
I turned to thank ... but she was there no more!

Bewildered, agonised, tears in my eyes,
I raised my hands in lamentation's grief;
But as I did a sharp and painful vise

Riveted round the finger, like paint's leaf
Retreats to hardened oak, hardening further,
Still further, into gold—shaped like a wreath—

And on my finger, shining all a-gather:
The poet's ring to me vouchsafed through grace!*140*
Apollo's son—Apollo, leader and father,

At last! Onwards, upwards, to see that Face,
Which seeing renders even verse quite mute.
Oh God! Great God! Flay me as Marsyas was

Should I, presumptuous, step up, dispute
Your Glory—ever-living Architect
Of all, who put the Cosmos under foot;

And as words poets thread, refine, connect,
So you—with every living thing—did same:
Each DNA proclaims You God are Rex! *150*

Then as my heart shouted his glorious Name,
The gold ring enwreathing my finger glowed,
So that its severe pressure lessened, tamed

By power that from only one source is owed;
My will now wielded it, could summon up
That Spirit under which all heaven's bowed.

I raised the ring, knowing it would unwrap
Its mysteries: light filled the corridor,
Pushed past the last Door's blocking, fatal trap;

Ahead could see the Garden, and much more! *160*
Beside me Saint Luke, the ox-headed man,
Strolled leisurely, who knew beyond the Door.

Outside, sunlight—Apollo's—so bright, shone;
Air fresh, reviving so, from that dull air
Within which I had breathed, death for so long.

How those divine rays bleached my skin and hair,
So that in all things I felt renewed, despite
My knowing that where Luke dug still was scarred.

An odd sound, and then I laughed—not with fright—
But there a pond where small ducks paddled, quacked; *170*
As round they went, I blessed their blesséd sight;

So small, so perfect—ducks with baby ducks—
Content and happy in their smallest pool;
For them, too, no fate intervened, no luck:

Grateful to be themselves in His great whole.
Luke stooped and touched the water; how they came ...
As if they knew him friend to feed their souls.

Luke looked at me: I saw he felt the same—
God's energy, self-sufficiency He had
Displayed in miniature through the duck's frame. *180*

I loved the little beasts, how they were made,
But saw how these were one of infinite moulds
On which the world's foundations had been laid.

But then, whilst still in rapture's wrapt hold,
Luke with one gesture bid me view the pond;
For why, I could not think, yet viewed its cold

And silent depths, and emptiness beyond;
Or what I thought was empty—its clear sheen
At first reflected what was near and yond:

Only, Saint Luke beside, no longer oxen, *190*
But his face young, handsome, flaming, virile;
In the mirror at least he was a man!

I gasped—my eyes strayed or wanted the while
To see and check for myself what he looked like;
Somehow, I could not break my gaze's file:

For further than reflection's surface strikes
Now deeper, deeper I saw the living things,
Move here, move there, in depths, in heights, and spikes

Of being. I saw the sword, the Cherubim—
God save me!—waving, blocking my access,$_{200}$
And as I did, knew this agent of Him:

Apollo called or Uriel most blessed,
Who healed even as with fierce heat he smote—
Had driven from Paradise at God's behest

That Eve and Adam lost, adrift, afloat
From goodness, truth and all beauty's bright sun:
To live on Earth in saucy fears and doubts,

Denying at every turn that always One;
Who now looked back—the pool no less His eye,
Piercing my heart until it was unspun$_{210}$

And dispossessed from its dense mystery.
I almost toppled, as one in sudden start
About to drown, now sees the scale of lies—

My own—but Luke's always present art
Held me back, said, 'Look deeper, deeper still.'
Beyond the flaming Cherubim's hard hurt

I glimpsed at her—she—the one I loved still:
Her blue eyes, face as rich as golden corn
When Ceres exults in summer, summer still.

I cried, 'My Lady Linda,' all forlorn. *220*
Then felt the ring a-humming on my finger.
'No time', I rasped. 'For her I must be gone,'

And broke my gaze away. 'No time to linger.'
I stood. How far was I from where she was?
All I knew was: my insatiable hunger

To see her again, and to see her face.
But how leave, go beyond this earthly Garden?
Luke knew my thoughts, and knew what was to pass:

'I have cut out your burden; Uriel then
Will withdraw his sword, freeing your progress *230*
To heaven which you desire to be in

And find your lovely Lady Linda, no less.'
'But how,' I said in panic, 'get so high?
Whither to go when StairWell itself ceases?'

He smiled. 'You have the ring of poetry:
Now high heaven is yours, for you can fly.'

NOTES

Epigraph. *non v'accorgete voi che noi siam vermi...* From a passage in Dante's *Purgatorio*, Canto X.124-29:

> Perceive ye not that we are worms, designed
>
> To form the angelic butterfly, that goes
>
> To judgment, leaving all defence behind?
>
> Why doth your mind take such exalted pose,
>
> Since ye, disabled, are as insects, mean
>
> As worm which never transformation knows?"

(Translated by Robert M. Durling)

CANTO 1: ASCENT

l. 87. *'Virgilius est nomen meum'*. 'My name is Virgil'.

l. 158. *'as Hezekiah prayed'*. In a famous biblical incident from 2 Kings 20: 1-11, Hezekiah prayed to God to be delivered from his illness:

> In those days Hezekiah became mortally ill. And Isaiah the prophet, the son of Amoz, came to him and said to him, "This is what the Lord says: 'Set your house in order, for you are going to die and not live." Then he turned his face to the wall and prayed to the Lord, saying, "Please, Lord, just remember how I have walked before You wholeheartedly and in truth, and have done what is good in Your sight!" And Hezekiah wept profusely. And even before Isaiah had left the middle courtyard, the word of the Lord came to him, saying, "Return and say to Hezekiah the leader of My people, 'This is what the Lord, the God of your father David says: "I have heard your

prayer, I have seen your tears; behold, I am going to heal you. On the third day you shall go up to the house of the Lord. And I will add fifteen years to your life, and I will save you and this city from the hand of the king of Assyria; and I will protect this city for My own sake and for My servant David's sake.'"'" Then Isaiah said, "Take a cake of figs." And they took it and placed it on the inflamed spot, and he recovered.

Now Hezekiah said to Isaiah, "What will be the sign that the Lord will heal me, and that I will go up to the house of the Lord on the third day?" Isaiah said, "This shall be the sign to you from the Lord, that the Lord will perform the word that He has spoken: shall the shadow go forward ten steps or go back ten steps?" So Hezekiah said, "It is easy for the shadow to decline ten steps; no, but have the shadow turn backward ten steps." Then Isaiah the prophet called out to the Lord, and He brought the shadow on the stairway back ten steps by which it had gone down on the stairway of Ahaz. (*NASB*.)

l. 181. *Uriel's.* Uriel means 'Light of God'. In Milton's *Paradise Lost*, Uriel is the Seraph who watches the Earth from the vantage point of the Sun. He is the keenest-sighted angelic being in Heaven; nevertheless, he fails to spot Satan's deception (*PL* III). In this sense he is one of the Cherubim or the Cherub who subsequently guards Eden from humanity's return. In Genesis 3:24, he is described as wielding 'a flaming sword which turned every direction to guard the way to the tree of life'. *The Book of Adam and Eve*, an apocryphal Old Testament text, additionally identified him as an angel of repentance. In Enoch 20:2 he watches 'over the world and over Tartarus' (trans. R.H. Charles, 1917). In the *Apocalypse of Peter*, he again appears as the angel of repentance, but is represented in an aspect as pitiless as a demon. His parallel with Apollo is due to the fact that both are Sun gods, and although Apollo is the god of poetry and prophecy, he is also the god of disease and destruction.

l. 201. *Like Eurydice, as blood in her sweet veins.* As she ascended from Hell, led by Orpheus, the wraith of Eurydice began gradually to assume bodily form. Indeed, she was almost fully re-composed into a physical human being when her husband made his tragic and fatal error by turning to check and see that she was still there.

l. 225. *pungi players.* A pungi is a Hindu reed pipe with a globular mouthpiece and often a drone, and so those who use it are snake charmers.

l. 246. *Like David dancing with the ark.* This is King David bringing the ark of the covenant of the Lord into Jerusalem for the first time since its long journey from Mosaic days (see 2 Samuel 6). The 'not condemning' him is an allusion to the fact that David's wife, Michal, did condemn him for dancing publicly; as a result, God made her barren.

l.286-7. *When as a listless shade I left you where / Man's Paradise begins?* This is a reference to Purgatorio Canto XXX where in the Forest of Eden Dante discovers that Virgil has quietly slipped away and that he will never see him again.

l. 323. *a second time.* Virgil traversed Purgatory a first time, enabling Dante to scale it in The Divine Comedy; now he will accompany Dante and the pilgrim for a second ascent.

l. 337. *Ahead, ten steps.* An allusion both to Hezekiah and the Ten Commandments —in crossing into Heaven all law must needs be fulfilled.

CANTO 2: FAMILY

l. 10. *'Scraping regret inherent in all Me'.* One story told of Satan is that he fell exactly at the moment when he uttered the word 'I' in the Divine Presence.

l. 18. *the Mantuan.* Virgil, who was from Mantua in Italy.

l. 41. *feeling where he rubbed the fig.* Another Hezekiah reference: 'Then Isaiah said, "Take a cake of figs." And they took *it* and placed *it* on the inflamed spot, and he recovered' (2 Kings 20:7).

l. 51. *the golden bough.* In Virgil's *Aeneid*, Book 6, Aeneas must carry a golden bough in order to enter the underworld. It indicated a special privilege—which it does now as he enters Purgatory for the second time, only this time not to return to Limbo.

l. 53. *painless – the double death.* Because he is in Limbo, not Hell proper, Virgil is not only excluded from Heaven (a first death), but aware of his loss (a second death). Whilst this is painless, nevertheless, his sense of loss is doubled.

l. 172. *Mother killed me.* Her own mother; the Poet's maternal grandmother.

l. 174. *Two brothers dead, just children, never men.* Two brothers, Denny and Jim, one dying at 5, the other 10 or 11. They died before the Poet was born, possibly through illnesses deriving from malnutrition.

ll. 175-6. *And I to be the same, only four years / Old, hospitalised—saving me for ten.*

The Poet's mother was hospitalised from aged 4 to aged 14 with TB, eyesight, and other problems.

l. 190. *He asked forgiveness as he lay dying.* Literally true, although in his final hour of life the Poet himself was the only one with his dying father—for one reason or another, other family members had been thwarted from being there. He died in a dreadful conflict, arguing with someone who appeared not to be there and in whom he did not believe; the Poet was terrified.

l. 243. *an angel on my shoulder.* A favourite expression regarding her 'luck'. She did live to 91 after all.

l. 295. *I knew that looking back was a mistake.* A faint allusion to Orpheus's mistake in Hell.

CANTO 3: EX-WIFE

l. 31. *There hell-bound, Herakles, son of Zeus.* As Odysseus discovers, the shade of Herakles was still in Hades even though his immortal spirit had been elevated to full godhead. Essentially, then, he is in two places at the same time! This phenomenon also occurs (though in reverse) in Dante in the *Inferno*: the soul of Fra Alberigo (Canto XXXIII) is in hell because of his deep treachery. His body is still alive on earth, however, but is possessed by a demon.

l. 48. *To flee His presence.* There are many references to this, but perhaps the most powerful one is to the prophet, Jonah:

> The word of the Lord came to Jonah the son of Amittai, saying, "Arise, go to Nineveh, the great city, and cry out against it, because their wickedness has come up before Me." But Jonah got up to flee to Tarshish from the presence of the Lord. So he went down to Joppa, found a ship that was going to Tarshish, paid the fare, and boarded it to go with them to Tarshish away from the presence of the Lord (Jonah 1:1-3).

Curious readers may be interested in my collection, *Inside the Whale*, in which being in the whale is the dominant metaphor for being swallowed inside a hospital. You can find out more here.

l. 56. *There idly lounging in its timeless waste.* Virgil was condemned for all eternity to remain in Limbo, not in pain, but not in the deep joy of heaven either.

Only when the blessed lady—Beatrice—came to visit him (*Inf.* II) did a new purpose for him activate itself and lead, as here, to a way out from the timeless waste.

l. 67. *Unlike Dante through whom light like bees swarmed.* Bees are especially redolent for Virgil. See his *Georgics*, Book 4.

l. 101. *As on a peak, wondering with fond surmise.* A nodding glance to Keats' great sonnet, "On First Looking into Chapman's Homer":

> Or like stout Cortez when with eagle eyes
> He star'd at the Pacific—and all his men
> Look'd at each other with a wild surmise—
> Silent, upon a peak in Darien.

l. 206. *The chair she sat on.* A nod to Shakespeare's *Antony and Cleopatra* (II.II.223-24):

> The barge she sat in, like a burnish'd throne,
> Burned on the water: the poop was beaten gold...

And its echo in TS Eliot's *The Wasteland*, line 77:

> The Chair she sat in, like a burnished throne.

l. 209. *Midas grants.* A legendary Greek king who was granted his wish to turn everything he touched to gold, which proved a dire curse.

l. 291. *Crassus.* A general of legendary wealth in the Roman Republic. His alliance with Pompey the Great and Julius Caesar fell apart after his death at the battle of Carrhae in 53 BC. It was reported that the victorious Parthians poured molten gold into his mouth to symbolically mock his thirst for money.

l. 367. *Hesperides.* The blissful garden at the western most point of the world, tended by three nymphs. The eleventh Labour of Herakles was to retrieve the golden apples from the garden. There are various versions as to how he did this, but one included slaying the dragon, Ladon, which guarded the apples.

ll. 402-7. *Why bring me out of the womb ... Perish the day my father blessed my birth.* A paraphrase from the Book of Job, especially 10:18-22:

Why then did You bring me out of the womb?

If only I had died and no eye had seen me!

I should have been as though I had not been,

Brought from womb to tomb.'

Would He not leave my few days alone?

Withdraw from me so that I may have a little cheerfulness

Before I go—and I shall not return—

To the land of darkness and deep shadow,

The land of utter gloom like darkness itself,

Of deep shadow without order,

And it shines like darkness.

CANTO 4: PEER

l. 44. *Octavian*. Anglicization of Gaius Julius Caesar Octavianus. After defeating Mark Antony at the Battle of Actium, he became Augustus, the first and greatest Emperor of imperial Rome.

ll. 52-3. *I praise the One I died ... Tiberius had no hold*. Virgil died during the reign of Augustus and before the birth of Christ. He accepts no responsibility for the acts of Tiberius, the second Roman Emperor under whom Christ suffered via his Governor Pontius Pilate. As a matter of fact, Dante himself thought Tiberius the third Roman emperor (*Paradiso* VI.88), since he counted Julius Caesar as the first.

l. 84. *Lex*. A body of laws that constitute how education is applied and operates.

l. 95. *Tubal-Cain*. A descendant of the murderer Cain mentioned in Genesis 4:22 who forged all instruments of bronze and iron; in other words, a blacksmith. But his importance is in the fact that he is an originator of technology that is invariably used for warfare.

l. 111. *siliconic*. A neologism meaning to be made of silicon.

l. 120. *Ness*. A contraction of Nessus, the famous centaur slain by Herakles. He manages to trick Herakles's wife into giving her husband a shirt soaked in his poisonous blood, and thereby gaining revenge as Herakles dies in agony when he puts it on. For my poem on the nature of love see, 'A Shirt of Nessus,' a villanelle, in my collection, *Rhythm and Rhyme at Storm*. You can find out more information about the collection here here. Also, see line 303 where the 'Shirt bloody...' is further developed.

l. 155. *TRISH.* An acronym for Technology Really Implementing Strategic Happenings.

l. 166. *Pelagius.* A British theologian born around 354 AD who clashed with St Augustine. Essentially, he denied original sin, and believed human beings were perfectible through their own efforts; in other words, he was an advocate of human progress through education.

l. 180. *shent.* Archaic word meaning 'put to shame or confusion'.

l. 192. *Hydra-poisoned arrow.* Herakles's second Labour was to destroy the Hydra. But one of the Hydra's heads was immortal. This one he cut off with a golden sword given him by Athena. Heracles placed the head—still alive and writhing —under a great rock on the sacred way between Lerna and Elaius, and dipped his arrows in the Hydra's poisonous blood.

CANTO 5: MENTOR-BOSS

l. 30. *As Rome on Pontine marshes.* Once a large, largely uninhabited malarial area near Rome. From the Romans to modern times, many from Augustus to Mussolini have sought to domesticate it. The point of the image is that Oxford spires go high, while Rome's Marshes go low; but either way, education and civilisation, whether up or down, is uncertain and insecure.

l. 32. *Cubicles, portacabins, structures temp.* These should resonate as permanent features for any visitor to UK schools.

ll.38-9. *not / Like that which Aeneas felt, or our gods rule.* In *Inf.* I.72, Virgil speaks of *nel tempo de li dei falsi e bugiardi*: 'in the time of the false and lying gods'. There is a clear distinction to be made between the experiences humanity has with the one God and those with pagan ones.

l. 44. *che lungamente m'ha tenuto in fame.* Dante, *Par.* XVIIII.26. The full quotation is:

solvetemi, spirando, il gran digiuno,

che lungamente m'ha tenuto in fame,

non trovandoli in terra cibo alcuno.

Breathe forth your words now, breaking at long last,

The fasting that has kept me hungering,

For food that I could never find on earth.

(Translated by Mark Musa)

For more on this topic, see my poem 'For Food I Could Never Find' in my collection, *Not Lost* (https://amzn.to/2S6G6Iu), which is a lyrical prequel to *The English Cantos*.

l. 76. *That moment the liar, dragon, just fell.* A reference to Satan. These few stanzas are an extended meditation on the Fall and its reversal through Christ.

l. 100. *How changed, oh utterly changed, I swear!* A reference to WB Yeats' 'All changed, changed utterly: / A terrible beauty is born' from his poem, *Easter 1916.* WB Yeats is the greatest poet of the Twentieth Century and one of my masters of style. Yeats did everything epic in his poetry, except write a full epic poem.

l. 115. Obliques - Persons who are oblique to the truth of reality.

l. 162-3. *and eyes of lust, / Lust of the flesh.* A reference to 1 John 2:16: 'For all that is in the world, the lust of the flesh and the lust of the eyes and the boastful pride of life, is not from the Father, but is from the world'.

l. 215. *No greater love than this.* A paraphrase of John 15:13: 'Greater love has no one than this, that a person will lay down his life for his friends'.

l. 255. *The Archer.* The zodiac sign Sagittarius, the Centaur archer.

l. ... *has no short arm.* A reference to 'Behold, the LORD'S hand is not so short That it cannot save; Nor is His ear so dull That it cannot hear.' (Isaiah 59:1)

l. 283. *Antares.* The largest star in the constellation of Scorpio, sometimes referred to as the heart of Scorpio, and some 700 times the size of our sun; a red giant.

l. 286. *an eagle broods.* Uniquely amongst the zodiac constellations, Scorpio is also represented by another symbol, the eagle: the symbol of death is thus also the symbol of resurrection. The essence of the Eagle is the clarity of insight and depth of penetration. Eagle's eyes see what others miss, discerning hidden motives, flushing out secret flaws and vulnerabilities. St John the Evangelist is always associated with the eagle.

CANTO 6: LOST FRIEND

l. 9. *I hungered for real food.* A line reminiscent of Dante's in *Par.* XVIIII.27: *non trovandoli in terra cibo alcuno*—'For food that I could never find on earth' (trans. by Mark Musa). This line inspired my poem, 'For Food I Could Never Mind,' to be found in my collection, *Not Lost*, https://amzn.to/32UhtAI

l. 18. *Seat.* As in 'seat of learning', usually designating a university or some such establishment.

l. 24. ... *a plumb rule / Plus mason's square*. A reference to a masonic tool kit: implements of rationality, derived from an Architect, but not from God.

l. 39. *Oz*. Referring most immediately to the Wizard of Oz, film and novel by Frank L Baum.

l. 54. And louder grew that voice - an echo of WB Yeats' refrain, 'But louder sang that ghost, "What then?"' from his poem, "What Then?"

l. 138. *Quietus*. Death, or something causing death or welcome release from life; or more generally something that calms or soothes.

l. 143. *Dryad*. In Greek mythology, a nymph inhabiting a tree or wood.

l. 182. *blow some seven times*. Recalling Joshua 6:1-27, where on the seventh day the Israelites marched round the walls of Jericho seven times, sounding their horns until its walls fell down.

l. 188. *Elohim!* One of the names of God given in the Old Testament, meaning possibly various things: Supreme or Mighty One, The Power over Powers, Strength or Might. This word for God appears in the very first sentence of the Bible.

l. 193. *Kastor's Double*. Kastor was the mortal twin brother of the immortal Pollux. The two were inseparable. When Kastor died, Zeus's decree brought them together in the zodiac star sign Gemini—the Twins. In one sense this can be construed symbolically as Kastor the body, and Pollux the immortal soul within the body.

l. 198. *Antaeus*. The giant and son of Poseidon. He challenged all-comers to a wrestling match, which he always won, as his strength was perpetually renewed by contact with mother Earth. However, he met his match in Herakles who, advised by Athena, held Antaeus aloft, draining his strength and crushing him to death.

l. 204. *Dioscuri*. Another reference to the Twins, Kastor and Pollux, meaning 'sons of Zeus'.

l. 207. *Cyllarus*. The name of the horse that Pollux tamed.

l. 231. *whose oozings crush*. An oblique recall of Gerard Manley Hopkins' poem, 'God's Grandeur,' and the line 'the ooze of oil / Crushed'.

l. 253. *And found a mirror*. Mirrors are always magical, and it was St Francis who observed that 'what you are looking for is what is looking'.

ll. 265-8. *Of Gemini .... Libra, Aquarius*. These are three astrological Air signs of the zodiac. If you think about them, they all share duality in their symbology: Gemini is a pair of twins, Libra is the two scales, and Aquarius is the man carrying water.

CANTO 7: FIGHTER

l. 28. *that other Day.* – the Day of Judgement, which is eternal, contrasting with human Emperors who judged ('thumbs-down') ephemerally.

l. 33. *another Sovereign's.* God's.

l. 99. *a thread.* A reference to the thread that saved Theseus's life when in the Minotaur's maze.

l. 110. *That dog.* Canis Major loyally follows its mythical master, Orion, the Hunter, across the southern skies of winter. The brightest star in Canis Major also is the brightest in the entire night sky — brilliant Sirius, which is just 8.6 light-years away. This dog of Dan Fast, too, has a certain glory.

l. 156. *not Kastor within but Pollux.* Pollux was the immortal twin and was famed for his boxing, whereas Kastor, mortal, was famed was his horse-taming.

l. 166. *said Virgil, 'in Limbo's arid jaw'.* It was from Limbo (Dante, *Inf.* III) that Virgil has escaped. His corporeal body is slowly reforming as he ascends.

l. 177. *The One who holds the Scales had turned the flood.* The Scales are Libra. See Milton (*PL* IV.996-1003), where Satan is judged to lose the combat:

> The Eternal, to prevent such horrid fray,
>
> Hung forth in Heaven his golden scales, yet seen
>
> Betwixt Astrea and the Scorpion sign,
>
> Wherein all things created first he weighed,
>
> The pendulous round earth with balanced air
>
> In counterpoise, now ponders all events,
>
> Battles and realms: In these he put two weights,
>
> The sequel each of parting and of fight...

l. 214. *In ancient times the Masters knew their part.* This is adapted from the *Tao Te Ching*:

> Those who in ancient times were competent as Masters
>
> Were one with the invisible forces of the hidden.
>
> They were deep so that one cannot know them.
>
> Because one cannot know them
>
> Therefore one can only painfully describe their exterior.

(Trans. by Richard Wilhelm)

l. 227. *no adder in the path.* The constellation of the snake, Ophiuchus, is sometimes called the "anti-Orion," because this constellation is positioned diametrically opposite to Orion in the sky; Ophiuchus appears in early summertime just about where Orion will be a half year later, at the same time of night. Orion boasted no animal could defeat him—but to subdue his pride the scorpion did; Ophiuchus is often said to be the 13th zodiac sign and appears between Scorpio and Sagittarius. The Israelite tribe of Dan (Genesis 49:17) was represented by the snake; and the most famous Danite, who judged the tribes of Israel, was of course Samson—another warrior hero whose weakness led to his undoing.

l. 234. *the Belt's triple line.* Orion's Belt, or the Belt of Orion (also known as the Three Kings or Three Sisters) is an asterism in the constellation Orion. It consists of the three bright stars Alnitak, Alnilam and Mintaka.

l. 260. *Dividing my spirit, soul.* Hebrews 4:12: 'For the word of God is living and active, and sharper than any two-edged sword, even penetrating as far as the division of soul and spirit...'

CANTO 8: COVID PRIEST

l. 43. *the chapel of St Luke.* The Royal Bournemouth Hospital where the Poet suffered his surgery for cancer has a chapel of St Luke for prayer and restoration, and the Poet extensively went there to pray once he had regained his strength and could leave his sick bed. Of course, naming it the chapel of St Luke is particularly appropriate as Luke—author of the gospel and the Acts of the Apostles—is known (by St Paul) as the 'beloved physician' (Colossians 4:14). He is symbolized by a winged ox or bull—a figure of sacrifice, service and strength.

l. 102. *And pointing ceilingward he held an ankh.* The ankh symbol—sometimes referred to as the key of life—is representative of eternal life in Ancient Egypt; its shape is a circle atop a cross.

l. 115. *The constellation—Aries' shining ghost.* Aries symbolises the Ram or sheep, who with their false priests no longer have a shepherd, and so are set to be lost.

l. 125. *This place—like Ripon in the north—is closed.* Ripon Cathedral: its crypt had been open continuously to the public for prayer for 1349 years. Meaning: not closed for the Black Death, the Great Plagues, the Spanish Influenza, not to mention the various wars that England has been involved in since AD 672. But it was closed during Covid-19.

ll. 154-5. *that estate / Saint Paul informs us of.* According to 1 Corinthians 3:13, 'each one's work will become evident; for the day will show it because it is to be revealed with fire, and the fire itself will test the quality of each one's work'.

ll. 163-4. *A vaulting pillar just like one before that Moses / Saw.* Exodus 13:21 says,

> And the LORD was going before them in a pillar of cloud by day to lead them on the way, and in a pillar of fire by night to give them light, so that they might travel by day and by night.

l. 189. *The One whose own Word He cannot forswear.* 2 Timothy 2:13 says, 'if we are faithless, he remains faithful, for He cannot deny Himself'.

l. 190. *uprist.* My favourite usage of this word has to be from Coleridge's *The Ancient Mariner*: 'Nor dim nor red, like God's own head / The glorious sun uprist' (97-8). Bliss!

l. 199. *There Penny sat, re-clothed in white, and sane.* Faintly echoing the Book of Luke:

> And *the people* came out to see what had happened; and they came to Jesus and found the man from whom the demons had gone out, sitting down at the feet of Jesus, clothed and in his right mind; and they became frightened.

For the full story see Luke 8:26-39.

l. 220. *An Arch, all Marble, not far the great White Hall.* Marble Arch in London is, of course, close to Whitehall, the centre of the British government. Marble Arch itself was constructed to celebrate Britain's victory over Napoleon, but before its construction it was the site of Tyburn, where traitors were executed.

l. 227. *Atlas.* This Titan notoriously tricked Herakles into holding up the sky for him, but Herakles just as notoriously tricked Atlas in return. The trickery involved in politics is perhaps more significant than the strength!

CANTO 9: HERAKLES

l. 28. *Winston.* Winston Churchill, who led Britain in World War II and helped the world defeat Nazism and Fascism.

l. 31. *Europe's pygmies.* The European Union and specifically its bureaucrats in Brussels.

l. 52. *old Nick.* An informal way of referring to the Devil, and so the luck of the Devil.

l. 79. *You have a mask, my friend.* A reference to the compulsory wearing of masks during the Corona virus epidemic.

l. 80. *Downing-Street-think.* Downing Street in London is the official residence of the Prime Minster of the UK.

l. 129. *For what if the sinless One had once sinned?* It was St Augustine who observed that we must not say that Christ was unable to sin, but that He was able not to sin. In that statement is the essence of God's freedom, and also His sublime power.

l. 132. *old Chaos.* A reference to Milton (*PL* II), where the 'Anarch old' longs to bring back the primeval chaos before God established order and created light.

l. 140. *supreme and towering Dis.* The Roman equivalent of the Greek Hades, or god of hell or the infernal regions; it is both a place and a person. In *Inf.* IX, Dante and Virgil arrive at the city of Dis, which resists their entrance.

l. 143. *My Lord, my God.* the words of doubting Thomas (John 20:28) after he puts his hand into the wound of Christ and establishes that He has been resurrected from the dead.

l. 166. *I get the credit; afterwards, a gong.* That's how the British Honours system works: meritorious individuals are awarded by the monarch with what is colloquially called a 'gong'—an honour such as a knighthood (Sir/Dame) or a peerage (Lord).

l. 198. *save the NHS.* This was a very prominent slogan during the Covid epidemic, that we the British public should save the National Health Service (NHS). Nobody much seemed to question how curious it was that we should be saving our health service when the point of the health service was, and had always been, for them to save us, the public!

ll. 210-11. *they stood a tick / And then a tock, then fatally they dropped.* The still suppressed and repressed fact that so many are dying of the vaccinations, not the covid.

CANTO 10: TOILETS

Title. *Toilets*. A well-known anagram for a famous Twentieth century poet: TS Eliot whom his friends referred to as Tom.

l. 3. *Bemused by Purgatory's vatic embrace*. Dante smiles because he knows what the Poet doesn't; namely, they are about to enter the realm of the poets. Vatic means prophetic or oracular and poets are said to be that! Indeed, should be that!

l. 41. *Aden Broncs*. A lesser-known American poet who prides himself on the precision and exactness of his forms and meter.

l. 43. *Mohonk*. A famous American hotel founded by the Smiley Family in 1869, and located in the Hudson Valley in upstate New York. The author shared a fabulous meal there with the President of The Society of Classical Poets, Evan Mantyk (and their wives), in 2019.

l. 66. *For him too our Lord was nailed*. Fortunately, salvation does not depend on writing great or even good poetry.

l. 99. *Zeke*. Full name, Zeke Jock Manic (l. 147). An even lesser-known American formalist poet (than Aden Broncs); also paradoxically, a rigid Catholic whose ego and self-importance have taken over any sense of perspective. The dangers, perhaps, of too much learning.

ll. 130-3. *Where was the Yahweh Moses heard, and feared?* There seemed to the Poet a certain effeminacy and over-delicacy in Zeke's approach and prayers to God—a sort of ritualism that disembowelled its efficacy. Thus, the look at Moses—he lived to be 120 years old before he died (Deuteronomy 34:7).

l. 149. *For heaven and earth have both set their seal*. This is a paraphrase of what Dante claims for his own Divine Comedy in *Par. XXV.2*. No wonder, then, that Dante feels 'hues of red' (l. 152) as Zeke appropriates what is not proper for him to say.

l. 159. *Then chance, heaven relents, allows your shot*. Heaven allows you the poet's Laurel Wreath (or Crown) in due time. The Wreath, of course, that Dante himself was not allowed or given by his home city of Florence in his own lifetime.

l. 165. *I covet every man's scope and skill!* Again, now paraphrasing Shakespeare and sonnet 29: 'Desiring this man's art and that man's scope'. Also used in TS Eliot's 'Ash Wednesday' poem:

Because I do not hope

Because I do not hope to turn

Desiring this man's gift and that man's scope

I no longer strive to strive towards such things

(Why should the agèd eagle stretch its wings?)

l. 163. *Mary*. Mother of Jesus.

l. 180. *Saint Peter's keys*. St Peter traditionally held the keys to heaven, but as Christ himself said, 'In my Father's house are many rooms' (John 14:2). The Catholic way via St Peter is for Zeke, but the Poet is not going that way but via another Apostle: St Luke.

l. 191. *I interviewed Buonconte on the Mount*. Buonconte da Montefeltro, who meets Dante in *Purg*. V. A violent and evil man, he calls upon Mary for salvation just before falling to his death, and so is saved; as with the thief on the cross: Luke 23 and its allusion in l. 239.

ll. 195-6. *John Wilmot, / Lord Rochester*. We have met two minor American poets but now we meet a major poetic force from the English seventeenth century. Rochester (1647-1680) lived an entirely debauched life, but on his death bed repented.

l. 196. *unbelief's great poet*. The critic Vivian de Sola Pinto described Rochester as the 'great poet of unbelief' and contrasted him with Milton as the 'great poet of belief'.

ll. 199-201. *Worst part of me and hated...* An adaptation of lines from Rochester's poem, 'The Imperfect Enjoyment'.

l. 215. *Not royal lord who stood before his king*. Charles II, a fellow libertine.

l. 218. *He asked me to read him a special passage*. Rochester himself, on his death bed, asked Bishop Burnet to read him Isaiah 53, which so affected him that he converted to Christianity. The opening two verses run:

Who has believed our report?

And to whom has the arm of the Lord been revealed?

For He grew up before Him like a tender shoot,

And like a root out of dry ground;

He has no *stately* form or majesty

That we would look at Him,

Nor an appearance that we would take pleasure in Him.

l. 233-4. *Sheep-dumb, and dumber sheep damned to the slaughter; / Who threatened no words, nor voiced no relief.* Christ as the Lamb of God who takes away the sin of the world is well-known; less well-known are the lines from Isaiah 53:7:

> He was oppressed and afflicted,
>
> Yet He did not open His mouth;
>
> Like a lamb that is led to slaughter,
>
> And like a sheep that is silent before its shearers,
>
> So He did not open His mouth.

See also 1 Peter 2:23: 'and while being abusively insulted, He did not insult in return; while suffering, He did not threaten, but kept entrusting *Himself* to Him who judges righteously'.

l. 240. *'Remember me in your kingdom,' he said.* See Luke 23:43.

l. 251. *In vast valleys those dead might live again.* Alluding to Ezekiel 37:5, and also to TS Eliot's reference to them in 'Ash Wednesday'.

l. 267. *brazen horns.* A complex image involving the brazen altar of the Old Testament (Exodus 30:28, Psalm 43:4, and Malachi 2:13) and its usage as a place of propitiation through animal sacrifice. Horns allude to animals—bronze to the ability to endure as well as to have affront, that is, 'to be brazen about ...'. But horns also allude—back in the sixteenth and seventeenth centuries—to cuckolds; whilst possibly not one himself, Rochester was actively involved in cuckolding others. Through Christ, all the brazen qualities will transmute to gold.

l. 269. *Let all my works be dust.* Before he died, Rochester ordered all his writings to be destroyed, and today we only have what survived that fire: his mother was keen to carry out this request.

l. 293. *Macavity-like.* Macavity is the famous mystery cat who is always 'not there'—from TS Eliot's 'Old Possum's Book of Practical Cats'.

l. 298. *Even daring to eat a peach seemed to wrench.* In TS Eliot's 'The Love Song of J Alfred Prufock,' we learn that Prufrock, the persona, asks: 'Shall I part my hair behind? Do I dare to eat a peach?'

ll. 300-1. *she who died elsewhere—a wench / Committing fornication.* The epigraph to TS Eliot's poem, 'Portrait of a Lady,' is from Christopher Marlowe's play, *The Jew of Malta* (IV.I):

> Thou hast committed—

Fornication: but that was in another country,

And besides, the wench is dead.

l. 311. *John.* John Milton, telling Tom how to write great poetry.

l. 312. *Hail great master of English iambic flow!* Not an especially iambic line, but then Dante was Italian and didn't know English; furthermore, Milton himself was simply great at breaking the rules: 'Of man's first disobedience and the fruit'—the word 'first' in the first line is the first violation of iambic meter!

l. 315. *Like some phalanx of fiery power that stuns.* A creeping allusion to *PL* IV.979: '...sharpening in mooned horns / Their phalanx, ...'

l. 319. *Beside your own.* Great poets praise each other as do great saints: see St Francis and St Dominic in *Par.* XI. Note the contrast with Zeke's attitude.

l. 324. *No membrane, joint or limb, exclusive bars.* From *PL* VIII.623-6:

...we enjoy

In eminence; and obstacle find none

Of membrane, joint, or limb, exclusive bars;

Easier than air with air, if Spirits embrace, ...

l. 336. *What kind of line is 'April's cruellest month'?* Milton is mocking his inexact paraphrase of the opening line of Eliot's *TWL*. It is the quintessential perversion of Modernism: to hate the season that brings life, and so to regard life as a curse.

l. 341. *Those women wait.* Aside from the two women he did marry, Eliot notoriously led at least two others to come to expect he would marry them.

l. 382. *fascistic, imperial boot.* Aside from his awful and generally talentless poetry, Pound was a supporter of Mussolini and the Fascists in World War II and was convicted of treason after it. His literary supporters seem to think this a small matter, as if men of genius were exempt from mundane morality. Eventually, they secured his early release from prison.

ll. 398-9. *that magic of V – / His wife.* Eliot had two wives: Vivienne and Valerie. Certainly, the former proved a purgatory to him; and the latter may have provided him with the strength to ascend the steps upwards.

l. 418. *A third ring must be found.* A very faint echo of Tolkien and the three elven rings that create balance; which itself, of course, has a Trinitarian focus.

CANTO 11: AIR LIGHT

l. 13. *The ring I wear is one of great poetry.* In his mortal life Dante did not achieve the Laurel Wreath from his hometown of Florence, but Apollo has more than compensated for that in the afterlife. Interestingly, one night, nine months after he had died, he appeared to his son Jacopo di Dante in a dream. There he informed Jacopo where the missing 13 cantos of *Paradiso* were hidden. When asked by Jacopo if he lived, Dante replied, 'Yes, but in the true life, not our life'.

l. 25. *as on a white stone.* In Revelation 2:17, Christ says, 'To the one who overcomes, I will give *some* of the hidden manna, and I will give him a white stone, and a new name written on the stone which no one knows except the one who receives *it*.' Dante has received that white stone and only he knows his new name written on it.

l. 32. *Which brought down town and walls of Jericho.* The power of his poetry matches that power which brought down the walls of Jericho: Joshua 6:1-27.

l. 35. *Twins.* The constellation of Gemini.

l. 36. *Medusa Nebula's faint glow.* The Medusa Nebula is a planetary nebula in the constellation of Gemini.

l. 86. *sophist.* A term for the pre-Socratic philosophers of Ancient Greece. The word has now a negative connotation as in the word 'sophistry': a wrangling with words and concepts to establish truth whilst simultaneously perverting it.

l. 98. *Professor A.I. Flight.* A world-famous philosopher and notorious atheist who argued against the existence of God for decades until scientific evidence forced him to change his mind. He was then a theist rather than a Christian; his book on the topic was reviled by his erstwhile colleagues and fellow atheists.

l. 100. *Why, I critiqued Lewis without fear.* A reference to C.S. Lewis, the great Christian apologist and formidable debater. Flight had studied under C.S. Lewis.

l. 102. *and where's the beef.* An expression made famous in American Presidential debates. Essentially, where is the reality in what you are saying?

l. 179. *visibly.* Along with others they had encountered, Flight was still wrestling with the adverse consequences of his beliefs and life choices.

l. 203. *Blondin.* Charles Blondin (born Jean François Gravelet, 28 February 1824 – 22 February 1897) was a French tightrope walker and acrobat. He toured the United States and was known for crossing the 1,100 ft (340 m) Niagara Gorge on a tightrope.

l. 216. *Jacob's Ladder.* The Patriarch Jacob has a dream at Bethel, in Genesis 28:10-

19, '... and behold, a ladder was set up on the earth with its top reaching to heaven; and behold, the angels of God were ascending and descending on it.'

ll. 217-8. *one stone, as the Old / Has it, or one rock the New*. The stone is the pillow on which Jacob rests his head and which he uses for the pillar: 'So Jacob got up early in the morning, and took the stone that he had placed as a support for his head, and set it up as a memorial stone, and poured oil on its top' (Genesis 28:18). This is the Old Testament. And in the New Testament we have the Rock on which Christ builds his church, which is Cephas or Peter (John 1:42).

l. 228. *Professor I.M. Air*. Another world-famous philosopher who espoused Logic and atheism in equal measure; indeed, his own verification principles invalidated virtually everything meaningful, and sadly he never applied such principles to his own work.

l. 231. *A best-seller in sixty-six different versions*. The Poet confesses that sixty-six may not be the exact number of translations of this work, but as a number approaching the number of the Beast in Revelations (666), it seemed apt! (Revelations 13:18).

l. 236. *Hume*. David Hume (1711-1776)—famous Scottish philosopher, sceptic and atheist, and a founding father of the Enlightenment.

l. 249. *NDE*. A Near Death Experience. Such an experience is what sent the Poet on his own journey, commencing in Canto 1 of HellWard. Initially, the NDE had led Air to conclude that he should 'revise all his theories', and that there was more to existence than mere logic, but he quickly relapsed to his old views.

l. 251. *Red Light*. In his newspaper account of his NDE, Air says that, 'I was confronted by a red light, exceedingly bright, and also very painful even when I turned away from it.' He also says that his experience reminded him of Hume's, which according to Air was 'without regret' and even polite. This, however, may be contested: John Blanchard cites a woman who attended Hume on his deathbed, recording that when with friends Hume was cheerful 'even to frivolity', but when alone he was often overwhelmed with 'unutterable gloom'.

l. 263. *in four-minute's death*. Air's heart stopped for four minutes.

l. 268. *Like smoke on Mount Sinai*. 'Now Mount Sinai was all in smoke because the Lord descended upon it in fire; and its smoke ascended like the smoke of a furnace, and the entire mountain quaked violently' (Exodus 19:18).

l. 302. *Prince of Air*. Also known as Satan: 'in which you previously walked according to the course of this world, according to the prince of the power of the air, of the spirit that is now working in the sons of disobedience' (Ephesians 2 v 2). Pride, of course, is the pre-eminent vice of the Devil and we see this particularly in l. 296 when Air claims he is superior to Hume as a philosopher.

l. 309. *Cocytus.* In Greek mythology, the river of wailing or lamentation that flows into the river Acheron, on the other side of which is Hades or Hell.

l. 319. *as before for His disciples.* Christ on His resurrection appearing to His disciples despite their being in a locked room (John 20:19).

l. 335. *Where were you when I laid the earth's foundation?* This and the subsequent two questions come from Job 38.

l. 342. *not Tripos led.* The final honours examination for a BA degree at Cambridge University. Note that Air is an Oxonian, but Cambridge is recognised as valid by fair-minded Oxonians, after all, isn't it Oxbridge? Furthermore, the tripos comes from the meaning, 'a three-legged stool occupied by a participant in a disputation at the degree ceremonies.' Here we have Air's own secular trinity substituting for divine revelation.

l. 382. *No handle—lock—defaced the frame of wood.* As in William Holman Hunt's painting, 'The Light of the World,' the door of the heart can only be opened from the inside.

l. 389. *As Scorpio's sign appeared, abstruse, arcane.* As Dante was born under the sign of Gemini, the Poet is born under the Scorpio sign, and the portent of heaven is also a portent of his own particularity.

CANTO 12: ST LUKE'S CHAPEL

l. 17. *the Word.* The Bible, and its ultimate source, the Incarnate Logos.

ll. 19-20. *if what be true is heard / And acted on, we knock.* A reference to Matthew 7:7: 'Ask, and it will be given to you; seek, and you will find; knock, and it will be opened to you'.

l. 27. *To where my whole fate could not be unlocked.* At this point one's salvation is no longer a matter of doubt: Romans 8:30, 'and these whom He predestined, He also called; and these whom He called, He also justified; and these whom He justified, He also glorified.' See also, Ephesians 1:11, 'In Him we also have obtained an inheritance, having been predestined according to the purpose of Him who works all things in accordance with the plan of His will.'

l. 32. *Appearing when all the doors were shut firm.* From John 20:19,

> Now when it was evening on that day, the first *day* of the week, and when the doors were shut where the disciples were *together* due to fear of the Jews, Jesus came and stood in their midst, and said to them, 'Peace *be* to you'.

A contrast here, though, for whilst Christ appeared in his glorious resurrection body, the Poet is unexpectedly back on the operating table.

l. 37. *Like I'd been drugged.* As indeed the Poet had been, anaesthetised on the table before the operation.

l. 40. *A pattern forming.* The pattern forming are all stars from, or around, the Taurus constellation, the opposite and antagonistic sign to Scorpio. The Poet has seemingly reverted to his old carnal condition, which is death.

l. 54. *Luke.* St Luke the Apostle, doctor and healer. See the first note on Canto 8, l. 43, for more on the ox's head.

l. 54. *I'm your lover.* See Luke 10:27: 'And he answered, "You shall love the Lord your God with all your heart, and with all your soul, and with all your strength, and with all your mind; and your neighbor as yourself."' Luke is the Poet's true neighbour.

l. 90. *But studio where her art healed all harm.* Check yourself for all its beauties: https://www.linda-sale-fine-art.com/gallery.

ll. 110-11. *all my engines inside,/ My brain itself is in this desperate torpor.* Following 2 major five-hour operations, the Poet had about 30% of his small intestines removed.

ll. 144. *Marsyas.* A satyr who challenged the god Apollo to a musical contest and lost, and so was flayed alive. His sin was the Greek sin of hubris in presuming to be as good as the god.

l. 150. *Each DNA proclaims You God are Rex.* That the intricacies of creation, especially the DNA code of living creatures, trumpet the fact that God is King, since the creation of life is beyond chance, accident or evolution. Evolution, of course, merely being chance multiplied to impossibility.

l. 170. *a pond where small ducks paddled, quacked.* A small detail recalled by the Poet as his strength to recover from the operations resurged, and he stepped outside for the first time: at the Royal Bournemouth Hospital there is a small pond where just such ducks quack!

l. 207. *in saucy fears and doubts.* A reference to Macbeth III.IV: 'But now I am cabined, cribbed, confined, bound in / To saucy doubts and fears.'

l. 219. *Ceres exults in summer.* For more on 'gracious Ceres' see Virgil, G I. And also, possibly, Keats in 'To Autumn' with his reference to plenty: 'Who hath not seen thee oft amid thy store? ...'

l. 223. *And broke my gaze away. 'No time to linger.'* A faint echo of a line from Gerard Manley Hopkins' sonnet, No Worst, There Is None:

... Fury had shrieked 'No lingering! Let me be fell: force I must be brief.

l. 227. *earthly Garden.* As he approached the summit of Purgatory, Dante too arrived in the Earthly Paradise (Purg. XXVIII-XXXIII), the Garden of Eden as it was—but not yet Heaven itself.

FURTHER REFERENCES

New American Standard Bible. (2020.) The Lockman Foundation, La Habra, CA.
(Original translation published 1971)

Abbreviations used to indicate sources:

NASB New American Standard Bible
PL Paradise Lost
Inf. Inferno
Purg. Purgatorio
Par. Paradiso
TWL The Wasteland
G Georgics

ABOUT THE AUTHOR

James Sale has been a writer for over 50 years, and has had over 40 books published, including 10 collections of poetry, as well as books from Macmillan/Nelson (The Poetry Show volumes 1, 2, 3), Pearson (York Notes : Macbeth, Six Women Poets), and other major publishers (Hodder & Stoughton, Longmans, Folens, Stanley Thornes) on how to teach the writing of poetry. Most recently his poems have appeared in the UK in many magazines. James was a co-founder and director of the KQBX Press, which published dozens of poets before it closed in the late 90s. Finally, the Bournemouth Yellow Buses company selected James as one of their top six poets as part of their marketing campaign around the town in 2016. He was given a free bus pass as part of the deal – nice! He won 2nd Prize in The Society of Classical Poets (New York) 2014 Annual Poetry Competition and First prize in their 2017 competition and was invited to join their Advisory Board. He was nominated for a Pushcart Poetry Prize by The Hong Kong

Review in 2022. He has had over 500 blogs published, many on literary themes and reviews, online as well as in magazines; he is an accredited 'Diamond Author' – their highest level – with ezine.com, the world's largest online article provider. James is also a commissioned feature writer on culture and poetry for New York's Epoch Times and recently has become a writer on culture for New Jersey's The Politeia. View all posts by james66dante

ACKNOWLEDGMENTS

Extracts from The English Cantos have appeared in the following magazines:

The Lowestoft Chronicle

The Society of Classical Poets

Especial thanks go to:

Joseph Sale for his critical perception and suggestions, as well as his editorial support

Linda E Sale, the artist, for her outstanding artistic contributions, including the covers

Evan Mantyk for his Foreword to StairWell and for publishing extracts in The Society of Classical Poets

Andrew Benson Brown for his unreserved support and critical acumen

Michael Pietrack for telling everyone in Colorado (and beyond!) about the poem

Professor Antonino Chiaramonte for discussing Dante with me

Angela Perrott, Judith Warbey and Mark Burden for their artistic interpretations of HellWard and StairWell

Colin and Liz Gilbey, Paul and Judith Denholm, Stuart and Pat Yates, David and Helen Orme for their unremitting friendship and encouragement of the project

And thank you to all the readers of my poetry who have helped spread the word about its authority, power and beauty. I really appreciate you all.

CONTRIBUTORS TO THE WIDER CIRCLE

Joseph Sale – Novelist, Writer, & Editor, Linda E. Sale – Artist, Robert Monaghan – Film Director & Game Designer, Evan Mantyk – President of the Society of Classical Poets, Pat Yates – Quaker, friend, and poetry enthusiast, J. Simon Harris – Poet & Translator, James B. Nicola – Poet, Steve Feltham – www.choralifiscus.org, Pascoe Sawyers – DJ & Author, J. D. Wallace – Professor of Communication Studies, Theresa Rodriguez – author of *Jesus and Eros: Sonnets, Poems and Songs*, David Orme – retired children's writer and religious art enthusiast, Angela Perrett – Artist, Judith Warbey — Artist, David B. Gosselin – a student of classics and languages based in Montreal, T. M. Moore – poet and Principle of The Fellowship of Ailbe, Brian Jenner – Speechwriter, Author & Event Organiser, & Sue Kerr – Art collector. Andrew Benson Brown – Poet. Judith Warbey – Artist. George Cochrane – Artist. Francis Etheredge – Catholic Theological Writer and Speaker . Timothy Schmalz – Sculptor. Leonardo Ramirez – Author & Screenwriter. James A. Tweedie – Poet. Sally

Cook – Artist & Poet. Anthony Watts – Poet. Glynn Young – Poet. Daniel Fitzpatrick – Novelist & Translator. Simon J. Harris – Writer & Translator. Antonino Chiaramonte – Electroacoustic Composer, Sound Designer, Live Electronics Performer and Flautist. David Russell – Editor.

Printed in Great Britain
by Amazon

19004750R00130